Praise for *Orphan Island*

A National Book Award nominee

An ALA Notable Children's Book

A Chicago Public Library Best of the Best

A 2017 Nerdies Middle Grade Fiction selection

A Bank Street College of Education
Best Children's Book of the Year

"Laurel Snyder has written a story that curls around the heart and pulls in tight—a meditation on the power and wisdom and closeness and sorrow of childhood. A wondrous book, wise and wild and deeply true. I loved every second of it." —KELLY BARNHILL, Newbery Medal–winning author of *The Girl Who Drank the Moon*

"So often (too often?) children's books do all the heavy lifting FOR their child readers. Almost as if they don't trust kids to make their own answers. We adults are so fond of our certainty these days. But when you're uncertain about something you have the capacity to learn. Kids have the capacity to learn, and *Orphan Island* gives them that. Laurel Snyder has handed them the gift of uncertainty and in this day and age it's a treasure precious. And rare."—ELIZABETH BIRD, A Fuse #8 Production

"Snyder, with her engaging and lucid prose, gets to the core of what makes the human heart beat faster, be it terror or love. *Orphan Island* is full of adventure, delight, tenderness, questioning, loss, fear of the unknown and the lure of it. This enormously appealing island paradise and its unexplained mysteries will leave readers begging for more."
—SHELF AWARENESS

"*Orphan Island* is a masterpiece—both timeless and immediate. Snyder's book, like the island within it, contains all of the joys, wonders, and terrors of childhood. Every young reader needs this book; every grown reader needs it even more." —JONATHAN AUXIER, *New York Times* bestselling author of *The Night Gardener*

"Through the precocious Jinny, Snyder delivers a contemplative commentary on the transition from childhood to adolescence, and from ignorance to awareness." —*PUBLISHERS WEEKLY* (starred review)

"A visionary, poignant, astonishingly lovely fable of childhood and change. This is a book to lose yourself in and to never forget."
—ANNE URSU, author of *The Real Boy*

"Snyder's tribute to the painful aspects of growing up is elegant in its simplicity." —*THE HORN BOOK*

"A gentle coming-of-age tale of children finding their own answers."
—*STAR TRIBUNE*

"This charming, engrossing tale set in a vividly realized world is expertly paced and will appeal to fans of wilderness adventure stories and character-driven relationship novels alike." —*KIRKUS REVIEWS*

"The premise is intriguing, the writing is strong, and the tight pacing will keep readers fully engaged." —*SCHOOL LIBRARY JOURNAL*

"An elegant and thoughtful meditation on the joys and sorrows of growing up, with lyrical prose, characters that feel as alive as your dearest friends, and a vivid setting sure to enchant young readers. A work of extraordinary heart." —CLAIRE LEGRAND, author of *Some Kind of Happiness*

LAUREL SNYDER

ORPHAN ISLAND

WALDEN POND PRESS
An Imprint of HarperCollins*Publishers*

Walden Pond Press is an imprint of HarperCollins Publishers.
Walden Pond Press and the skipping stone logo are trademarks and registered trademarks of Walden Media, LLC.

Orphan Island

www.harpercollinschildrens.com

ISBN 978-0-06-244342-7

Typography by Amy Ryan
18 19 20 21 22 CG/BRR 10 9 8 7 6 5 4 3 2 1
❖
First paperback edition, 2018

For Emma, my island

We could never have loved the earth so well if we had had no childhood in it.

—George Eliot, *The Mill on the Floss*

Contents

Orphan Island

1

Bell and Boat

Jinny heard the bell. She threw down her book, rose from the stale comfort of the old brown sofa, and scrambled for the door. When she burst from the cabin into the evening air, Jinny *ran*.

Along the beach, everyone was running—bolting for the cove, summoned by the golden clatter of the bell, so bright in the dusk. Eight kids, sprinting from the fire circle or the outdoor kitchen, emerging from their cabins, racing for the bell and the tall boy ringing it by the water's edge.

It was like this every time the bell rang.

At the cove, they lined up, breathless and staring out to sea, to watch the boat come in against the sunset. They stood waiting like uneven fence posts. There was Deen, who towered beside Jinny and now leaned to set the bell gently back on its hook, and little Sam, beside him. There was thin Eevie, frowning at the lapping water as though it had done something wrong, and Oz and Jak, jostling each other. Joon stood tall and straight at one end of the line, her gaze intent on the sea, and Nat waited patiently beside her, a book clutched in her hands. Then there was Ben, just a year below Jinny and almost exactly her height, smiling his easy smile as he stared out at the water patiently.

Deen had been the one to spot the small green boat, appearing through mist that wreathed the island, cutting through the whitecapped waves. Deen had lifted the bell and rung it to summon the others. Deen had been alone, briefly, with the knowledge that it was time again for a Changing.

Jinny didn't think that was fair to Deen. After all, it was his turn to leave. He shouldn't have had to ring the bell too and stand there on the beach, waiting alone. Jinny edged closer to him now. She took his cold hand, and Deen gripped her fingers tightly, laced them with his own, but didn't turn to look down at her. He kept his dark eyes trained on the boat in the distance, so Jinny did the same. She wondered what he was thinking. He seemed strangely calm, unsurprised, almost like he'd been waiting for the boat. But his jaw was clenched firmly.

In a handful of silent minutes, the boat slipped into the cove and nestled its green prow in the sand at their bare feet. Then came the empty *before* moment. The strange heartbeat of time when the nine kids on the shore peered into the boat. Before anybody said a word. They all stared.

At the shivering child staring back.

Jinny knew she should be the one to speak first, to reach out a hand and help the kid onto the island. This one would be hers, after all. Her Care. Jinny was oldest after Deen, and would officially become Elder the moment he stepped into his boat. But she couldn't seem to move her feet. She didn't feel ready. Jinny curled her toes into the damp sand and squeezed Deen's fingers. He squeezed back but then let go. Leaving Jinny's hand lonely. She dropped it to her side.

Last year there had been a boy in the boat, yellow-haired Sam, who now stood on the other side of Deen, sniffling. Always sniffling. Sam had belonged to Deen, had stumbled along after him like a shadow wherever he went. Sam had shared Deen's sleeping cabin and been always underfoot, learning the island from the tall boy who would be leaving now, so suddenly.

This new arrival was a girl, of course. It was a girl year. Her eyes were huge in her face, stunned. Her chin trembled, and her black curls were damp with sea spray. The girl was pretty, but that didn't matter. Really, kids all looked the same sitting in the boat. Boy or girl, fat or thin, dark or light. They looked damp, lost, and snot faced. The salt spray made their noses run.

Now everyone was waiting. Waiting for Jinny to say

something. She was taking too long and she knew it, but it was hard to speak. She was frozen in the moment she'd been dreading for hundreds of sleeps. At last she forced herself forward. Her feet stuttered in the sand as she reached one arm stiffly into the boat, hand open, palm up.

"Hey!" she called too loudly. Her own voice rang in her ears. "What's your name?"

The girl stared at Jinny's hand. She opened her mouth and looked around, out and down the beach, then back at Jinny and the line of curious kids. The new girl shook her head ever so slightly.

"Oh, come on," said Jinny. "There's nothing to be afraid of. Get out!" She didn't want to have to reach in and grab. She didn't want to scare the girl any more than she was already scared. Everything would be so much easier if she stepped out on her own.

The new girl stared at Jinny for a few frightened breaths, a few ripples in the shallow surf. Everyone waited. At last she spoke. "Mama?" she asked, staring wide-eyed at Jinny.

Jinny shook her head. "No," she said. "No mama. We don't have mamas here. But it'll be okay. I promise. You just need to climb out. *Now.*" She didn't mean to sound heartless, but the new arrivals always did this at first. Soon enough, the girl would forget about *mama*. She would come to understand—the island was instead. The island was better.

The girl squeezed her eyes shut. So Jinny took a deep

breath and stepped forward, leaned in. She put a foot in the boat, and the girl cried "Ah!" as the boat shifted and shook slightly with Jinny's weight. But it didn't drift. The boat never drifted.

Nobody had any idea how the boat worked. It arrived at this same spot, through the thick mist. As if pulled by an invisible string. Then it left again, a few minutes later, the same way. The boat was as reliable as anything, as sure as the stars.

Jinny reached for the girl. Gripping her under her thin arms, Jinny dragged her forcibly from her spot on the plank seat and up over the green side of the boat, and then swung the girl up onto her hip, so that she could carry her awkwardly back to the line of children, where she plunked her down heavily in the sand. Harder than she meant to, so that the kid let out a startled "Uhhf!"

After that, Jinny pushed the girl from her thoughts, because it was *time*. The boat was empty. Waiting. Jinny turned to look at Deen and frowned. "Are you . . . ready?"

Deen nodded. His lank hair shook in his face. "Guess so," he muttered. "I guess it's time, huh?" He stepped forward and turned around to face them. He glanced up and down the line—at all of them.

"Well," Deen said. "So . . ."

Jinny heard a choking cry as Sam broke from the line and ran forward, burying his face in Deen's belly. Deen reached down and placed a sturdy hand on Sam's head but kept talking.

"Hey, hey—I'll miss you, buddy. But there's no need to cry. I'll see you all again, on the other side. When your turn comes. Right?"

Nobody answered him, but behind Deen, the boat rocked impatiently. Deen crouched down to hug Sam. "I have to go, Sam-man," he said. "But you'll be okay. The others will take care of you." He looked back over his shoulder at Jinny, as if for help. But his voice was flat, as it had been so often lately. As though he was reciting the words. They didn't feel *true*, exactly. They didn't feel like he meant them, not the way he should.

Before Jinny could react, Ben stepped forward. He walked surely down the line of kids, lifted Sam in a hug, and carried him wordlessly away. Even as Sam sobbed, Ben didn't stumble. He walked steadily back toward the path and the cabins. It was wonderful, Jinny thought, how Ben always seemed to know just what to do. Ben was so good. She wondered what it felt like to be always so good.

Anyway, it was just as well Sam left, thought Jinny. Nothing would make the next few moments any easier for him. And how many times could a person say good-bye? Eventually the sun would slip into the sea. Deen had to climb into the boat before it got too dark. Everyone knew that.

One by one, the other kids followed Ben's lead. They hugged Deen good-bye and choked back their tears, or didn't, and straggled back to their cabins. To eat or read or climb under their covers and sleep heavily. It would be a silent night. It always was. Deen didn't cry, so Jinny willed herself not to.

At last the others were gone, and Jinny and Deen stood alone together, beside the new girl, a tiny heap of person in the sand. So silent she almost wasn't there. Deen was still frozen, rigid and staring *out*, so Jinny reached up to hug him for the last time, wishing he'd soften, melt into his old self. She buried her face in his neck. She set her cheek against the sharp angle of his collarbone, so that his hair tickled her cheek. She waited for him to speak first. Her best friend. Her brother. But he didn't speak. He only pulled away, backed out of her hug.

"Oh," said Jinny.

Deen was the only person left in her world who'd been here when Jinny had arrived. She couldn't remember that day, and she doubted he could either, but it still meant something. For as far back as she could recall there had been Deen, exactly a head above her. Her constant companion. Now he was leaving, and *she* would become Elder, the tallest tree, with the longest memory. She didn't feel ready.

The mercy of a Changing was that the little ones never remembered their own arrivals. Often they even forgot their Elders as the years slipped by, all the hours spent, all the lessons learned together. The memories floated away with the sleeps.

Jinny could barely recall Emma, her own Elder. She only remembered a blur of red hair and freckles, a soft breathy laugh. A tall person, holding her hand so tightly that her finger bones hurt when they climbed the boulders to the cliffs, side by side. In the same way, Sam might now forget Deen. It was hard to believe that could happen, but they were so young when all this took place. What they knew—*all* they knew—was the island itself, years of running on the beach, singing by the fire, plucking fruit from the trees and fish from the nets. Salt and sand and sun. They only knew the good of it.

But for Jinny, *this* Changing would be different. This moment would never fade for her. She knew that, inside herself. She could feel it being etched into her memory. She hoped Deen felt the same. She looked at him and memorized his face—smooth skin, with the cheekbones sharp beneath them. Had he *always* looked like that? Jinny didn't think of Deen as sharp. When had that happened?

Jinny memorized the feeling of the moment too—the grit of damp sand beneath her scrunched toes, the lapping of the surf, the salt on her lips. She licked them. Deen could pretend not to care, but she refused.

"I don't want you to leave," Jinny said, shaking her head.

Deen forced a smile. "Well, for once you don't get what you want."

Jinny frowned at him. "Don't say that. It's not funny."

"It'll only be a year," Deen said. "Then I'll see you again." He glanced down now, made eye contact.

But something in what he'd said bothered Jinny, and she

spit out a mouthful of words that surprised them both. "You don't *know* that. You don't *know* where the boat goes. Nobody does. It could take you over the edge of the earth. Or into the jaws of some ravening sea creature, like in a book. It's nice to be cheerful in front of the littles, but really you could just sail off into the sea forever, until you wasted away from hunger. Couldn't you?"

Deen stared at her now, as though he didn't quite recognize her. "Well, that's a happy thought," he said tightly.

"Maybe I shouldn't have said that," said Jinny. "But you know it's the truth, and you don't seem to care. It's almost like you *want* to go away. Or like you're already gone. Like you've *been* gone. Why?"

"Cut it *out*," said Deen. He kicked at the side of the boat. "It's not that simple, Jinny. I can't explain . . . how this feels. Not even to you. You wouldn't understand."

"Try me," said Jinny.

Deen shook his head. "I don't know how. Anyway, I *have* to get into the boat. Why do you want to go and make it harder for me? Why do you want to fight *now*?"

Jinny's mouth snapped shut, and her eyes darted to the sand. Was that what she was doing? She hadn't meant to. She had only wanted him to care. . . . "I'm sorry," she muttered. "I'll just miss you is all. A *lot*."

"Of course you will," said Deen. "And me too. But it's not like I have a choice in this. You know?"

Jinny bit her lip, trying not to say the wrong thing again. But she couldn't keep silent. "Well, maybe you *do* have a choice. I mean, you could . . . stay."

"Stay?" Deen squinted.

Jinny nodded, glancing back up at him.

"You know I can't do that, Jinny," said Deen.

"Why not?"

"Because." Deen's voice was gruff now, angry. "You know the words." Then he recited:

> *"Nine on an island, orphans all,*
> *Any more—"*

Jinny cut him off with a sharp laugh. "*The sky might fall?*"

Deen shrugged. "That's how the song goes. . . ."

"The thing is," said Jinny, "skies don't actually *fall*. Just look at it." She craned her neck, stared up into the reliably endless expanse overhead. "Did you ever see something so *permanent*? It's just a silly little song. Who knows who even made it up? Probably some Elder years back, to entertain their Care. I could make up a song too, if I wanted. I could even rhyme if I tried." She thought for a moment, then added, "Like this:

> *"Everyone must go away,*
> *Except Deen. Yes, Deen should stay."*

Jinny stopped singing. "There! How's that? *Now* will you stay, since it rhymed and all?"

Deen shook his head, exasperated. "Listen, Jinny, the island has rules for a reason. We have to follow them. Remember what happened the time Tate picked all the curlyferns, even though everyone knows you're never supposed to pick the last of anything, ever? And then they never grew again? We were so mad at her! Remember how good those ferns were, and now they're gone."

"That's different," said Jinny. "*That* rule made sense. This one doesn't."

Deen wasn't looking at her anymore. He was turned away again, staring down at the green boat. "Stop it, Jinny. This is the way it works. I have to leave. And next year it will be *your* turn. So you'd better get used to the idea. What would happen if we all just stayed forever?"

"I don't know," said Jinny. "And neither do you. It might be fine. . . ."

"But it might not," argued Deen. "And what if the sky did fall? What if it broke to bits?"

"Skies don't break, Deen."

"Enough, Jinny!" Deen's voice was loud now, and suddenly deeper than she'd ever heard it. Deen didn't sound like himself. He sounded harder, older. "The boat comes when the boat comes. You can't just do whatever you feel like all the time. And anyway . . ."

"Anyway *what?*" asked Jinny.

"Anyway . . . ," said Deen, "I might be ready . . . for something else. Did you ever think of that? That I might be curious what's out there?" He looked at the sea beyond the boat and squinted. "Aren't you? At least a little bit? Don't you want to see what more there is?"

Deen's last sentence hung in the air between them for a long moment before Jinny said, "Oh." She looked down at her dirty feet in the sand. "Well, if you *want* to go, that's different. Don't let me stop you."

"You'll understand," Deen said, stepping away from Jinny. "You will, when it's your turn. It's . . . different. You'll change too."

Jinny shook her head. She didn't say anything. What could she say to that? If she tried, she knew she'd cry. Deen *had* changed. He'd been odd for sleeps and sleeps, and she hated it.

Deen waded into the surf. "I'm done talking about this," he said as he turned to the boat. His back was to Jinny. "I'll see you, when you come." Without even glancing over his shoulder again, he shouted, "Bye!"

"No, Deen, wait!" Jinny cried. Deen couldn't leave like that. Fighting. He wouldn't.

But that's exactly what he did do. Because the minute he sat down on the low plank seat, the green boat backed up into the cove and then turned and zipped away. In a true straight line, quickly out into the open water, back to wherever it came from. No different from any other year. The boat didn't know they were fighting. The boat didn't give them an extra minute to make up. The boat had someplace to be.

As he sped off, Deen turned to look back at her over his shoulder. He called out something. But what? Jinny could see his mouth open and close. He threw a hand sharply into the air, but whatever he said was lost in the spray and mist as they swallowed him.

Jinny watched the boat disappear. Until all she could see was water and distance. It happened so fast. She found herself standing, reaching out both arms, in the direction the boat had gone. Both hands with outstretched fingers, grasping. As if there was something in the air she might be able to clutch.

2

Two Sad Shapes

Jinny dropped her hands to her sides. Her last moments with Deen had been the absolute wrong last moments. The worst last moments she could imagine. She had never felt so lost. Or tired.

Only then did she remember the lump on the sand. The new girl. She glanced over. The kid had been there, silent the whole time, watching with her big brown eyes. Jinny slid down into the sand beside her. "Well, *that's* a welcome for you, I guess," she said.

The girl didn't reply. Her chin was wedged between her knees. For some reason, that made Jinny want to do the same. She wrapped her arms around her legs, then poked her own chinbone down into her knees. It felt good, sharp. She hugged herself tightly and thought maybe she could remember sitting like this before, when she was younger. It felt familiar.

They sat together. Two sad shapes in the sand. Watching the day sink behind the cloudy sea. The oranges and pinks of the bleeding sunset made their usual swirling patterns above the mist, looping and arching. Tonight the shapes looked like dolphins. Or maybe just waves, calm soft waves. The new girl stared up, her mouth open slightly, saying nothing as she watched the sky shift and dance, a wash of shapes and colors.

Jinny took a deep breath, but it shook coming out. "You like that?" she asked after a minute, pointing at the sky. Her own voice sounded fragile to her, thin.

The girl didn't turn her head to look, but she nodded silently.

"Sunrise shapes are better," offered Jinny softly. "The pictures are clearer in the morning. You'll see."

Slowly at first, and then all at once, the shapes faded and the light drained from the sky. It was dark, but the two girls were still sitting in the sand when Jinny felt a small head of wet curls lean against her arm. The girl sighed deeply. It was a big sigh for such a small body. She set a hand on Jinny's foot.

Jinny was startled by the touch, and then she was crying silently. Hot fat tears dripped down her face. The girl stared at her in the shadows, watched her cry with that intense gaze. Jinny wiped her face against her arm, shook her head, and sat up stiffly. "I'm fine," she said. "I'm okay. Let's go!" She stood up, brushed the sand from her clothes; and when she did, the girl followed her lead.

Then Jinny realized—she wasn't doing her job at all. *She* was Elder now, and her Care must be tired. It wasn't the new kid's fault Deen had gone, or that he'd been so distant and strange before he left. Jinny put an awkward arm around the girl and gave her bony backbone a few hesitant pats. "Hey, you never told us your name. Do you have a name?" Jinny asked.

"Ess," said the girl softly.

"Well, then, are you going to tell me what it is?"

The girl tilted her head up. "Ess," she repeated.

"So, what *is* it?" asked Jinny.

Now the girl looked puzzled. "Ess!" she cried in a sharper voice. "Ess." She pointed at herself.

"Your name is *Ess*?" asked Jinny.

The girl frowned and shook her head. "*Ess*," she tried again.

"Bess?" This happened sometimes. The kids couldn't pronounce their own names. They were too young, with their soft, slippery little-kid tongues, lacking the hard consonants they needed. But it didn't matter. Soon enough they got used to their island name, whatever it turned into.

"Ess," repeated the girl, clearly frustrated.

"Okay," said Jinny. "Close enough. C'mon, Ess." Jinny didn't wait for Ess to answer her. She grabbed the girl's hand

and pulled her off down the beach, heading for the sleeping cabin the two would share until the boat returned.

Ess, snotty and stumbling behind her, hardly seemed a fair exchange for Deen. But now they could all take a deep breath and not think about the boat, for however many sleeps the year turned out to be. Things would go back to normal.

Jinny pulled Ess with her as she walked along the beach and into camp. There, Joon was banking the fire, her face glowing in the firelight. It was early yet, but the kids always skipped fire circle on the night of a Changing. Joon looked up as they passed, but Jinny didn't stop to chat or introduce Ess. There would be time for that in the morning. She only waved and headed straight up the sandy path, climbing the ridge to her own cabin.

Probably the others were together tonight, thought Jinny. Bunking together, whispering beneath the blankets. Oz and Jak. Nat and Eevie. Maybe Ben had stayed with Sam, after carrying him back to his cabin. It would be like Ben to do that.

Jinny and Deen had always bunked together on these strange nights. She remembered once, years back, she and Deen had snuck away on a Changing night and made a bed in the high grass of the prairie, with their blankets and pillows. When they'd woken up, there had been a mouse, chewing on the pillow between them, and Deen had screamed so loud that Jinny's ears rang. Jinny smiled, remembering how Deen had leaped from the ground, shaking his blankets in a frantic, goofy-looking dance. They'd never taken their pillows to the prairie after that.

Once inside the cabin, Jinny lifted the girl up onto the bed and pulled off her tiny shoes. It was early yet to go to bed, but Jinny was finished with the day. It had been plenty already. She'd do better tomorrow. She'd know how to handle it all in the morning. She hoped.

"Good night, Ess," she said softly. "Go to sleep."

But Ess didn't lie down. She just sat there on the bed and stared at Jinny, like she was waiting for something. Jinny wondered what it was she needed. Deen had told her he sometimes sang to Sam at night, but it felt odd to just start singing at the new girl. They didn't even know each other.

"Ummm . . . how about I get us some tea?" asked Jinny. "Mint tea. You want some?"

Ess didn't seem to exactly understand the question, but Jinny grabbed her mug from the bedside table anyway and said firmly, "Wait here." Then she opened the door and stepped out.

As she passed the door to Deen's cabin, she stopped. It struck her for the first time that it *wasn't* anymore. It *wasn't* Deen's cabin, and never would be again. It was Sam's cabin now. I need to see it, she thought, as she twisted her body to face the door, to open it slowly. I need to see it without him. She took a deep breath and peered inside.

"Hello?" she whispered.

"Jinny?" A small voice, alone in the darkness. Sam was awake. Ben hadn't stayed with him after all. The boy looked so tiny in the double bed. Pale, like a ghost, his blond hair against the pillow.

"Oh!" said Jinny. "Sorry. I didn't know if you'd still be awake."

"I don't *want* to be," said Sam. "I can't sleep. Why are you here?" He gave a sniff.

Jinny peered around, as if she might find an excuse for her presence on the floor or windowsill. Sam's and Deen's mugs were on the small bedside table. She looked down at the heavy mug in her own hand. "I, umm . . . I just thought I might . . . grab Deen's mug. That okay?"

"Sure," said Sam. "I guess so."

Jinny reached for the mug with her free hand, but once she was holding it, she found she wanted *more*. She wanted to take everything from this room, take it all back with her. Everything Deen had left behind. The collection of locust shells. His sleeping shift, hung on a nail by the door. She switched both mugs to the same hand and reached for the shift. "I'll just take this too, run it over to . . . the ragbag for you. Okay?"

"O-*kay*," said Sam. Though it didn't sound exactly okay to Jinny. She wished she knew better how to talk to him. She'd never quite figured out how to do that. She ruffled his hair instead, like Deen would have done. *G'night, Sam-man*, he'd say.

This whole long year, since the day Sam had arrived, Jinny had never really known what to say to the boy. That had been the day Tate had gone away, clambered into the green boat eagerly. *Tate* hadn't felt conflicted at all. She'd been ready, as she was always ready for an adventure, and *that* had stung Jinny. She remembered the moment, the burn of it, the tears in her eyes as she'd hugged her excited friend good-bye. But at least she'd still had Deen. . . .

How had it been so easy for them—for Tate and Deen? Jinny knew it wouldn't be like that for her. She wouldn't be able to just step into the boat, wave, and turn away. . . .

She should be better to Sam, she knew, try harder. It hadn't been his fault that things changed when he arrived. But it had *felt* a little like his fault. Deen had lifted him from the boat, just as Jinny had lifted Ess. Dangling the kid by his armpits, snot faced and sad. Then a moment later, Tate was gone. That had been the first night that Jinny and Deen hadn't sat up by themselves talking before bed, watching the stars from the path in front of their cabins.

Then there had been the following morning, when Jinny had showed up at breakfast and found Sam in her usual spot beside Deen. Right away, before Jinny even said a word, Deen had frowned at her. "He's little, and he's my *Care*, Jinny."

"Yeah, *Jinny*, got it? Eevie had echoed with a sneer.

Jinny had gotten it.

In his bed, Sam yawned, startling Jinny from her memory. "I'm tired now," he said. "All right?"

It was her cue. Clutching the mugs, with Deen's shift over her shoulder, Jinny turned to the door. "Well, okay then," she said. "I hope you get some good sleep tonight, Sam."

"I'll try," said Sam in a faint whisper. Then he added. "Hey, Jinny?"

Jinny paused. "Yeah?"

Sam's voice sliced through the darkness. "Are *you* okay?"

For a brief moment, Jinny paused before she reached for the doorknob. But only for a moment. "Yeah, I'm fine," she said quickly. "Totally fine. Good night, Sam."

Then she opened the door and ran, with the pewter mugs clanking. Down the path, letting herself fall downhill, so that gravity pushed at her, forced her to keep moving. So fast she couldn't have stopped if she'd wanted to.

The sky over Jinny's head was clear, and the stars were blazing as usual in the black sky. But they blurred as she ran down the sandy path to the dunes and the beach. It was lovely as ever, the hush of the island. The night breeze in the tall sharp grasses, the chirping and clicking of insects. It made Jinny feel better to run so fast, to be utterly alone in the familiar night. The grassy, sandy path still warm beneath her feet. *Everything* wasn't changing. Mostly, things were exactly the same.

Down on the beach, Jinny walked past the fire circle and the long wooden table and headed for Joon, who stood under the tin roof of the outdoor kitchen. At the cookstove, Joon stepped aside so that Jinny could reach for the rag-wrapped ladle. Once a day, someone filled the water pot with well water, so that it was always there, steaming and ready on the edge of the stove.

"She okay?" Joon asked as she rinsed the last few dinner dishes, abandoned by someone at the sound of the bell. "The new girl, I mean?"

"Oh, yeah," said Jinny. "I guess so. She's just sitting there on my bed, waiting. But I don't know what to say to her. She seems confused."

"Of course she's confused," said Joon. "We all were, at first. Probably."

"Well, sure," said Jinny. "But it's making *me* confused. And . . . I don't know. Sad."

"How could you not be sad, Jinny?" Joon's gaze was blunt, unsympathetic. "Deen was your best friend."

"I mean she's making me *sadder*," said Jinny, inhaling the steam from the hot water in the two mugs. "Or . . . Oh, I don't know what I mean. I just didn't know what to say to her. I thought I'd get us some tea."

Joon shrugged. "Tea never hurts. Here you go." She tore a clump of fresh mint leaves from the fragrant patch at her feet.

Jinny added the leaves to the steaming water and poked them under with a quick finger. Then she nodded good night and headed back up to her cabin, wishing silently that it had been Ben by the fire just now, and not Joon. Ben would have understood what she was feeling without her having to explain it. Ben would have given her a hug. Joon was fast and smart and strong, but not very huggy.

When Jinny got back to the cabin, she found Ess had conked out in her absence, tumbled right over on top of the blankets. Sprawled beside the window, the girl seemed to shine in the moonlight, her thumb in her mouth. Jinny reached out to touch her. "Ess?" she whispered. The girl looked so small in Jinny's bed. Her curls were still damp, and now so was the pillow.

Jinny took a sip from the mug in her hand. The tea burned the roof of her mouth, but somehow the burning almost felt good. Or it felt right. Jinny took another punishing sip and watched the girl sleep. Then she set down her mug, slipped into her sleeping shift, and pulled back the blanket at the foot of the bed.

The kids always slept this way, tip to toe, when they had a Care, with a pillow at each end of the bed. Jinny remembered when Deen had told her about that part. It had been the first Elder lesson of all. After his first night with Sam, he'd explained it. "So they can't drool on your face," he'd said. "But watch out for the kicking!" and Jinny had laughed out loud. It had seemed funny at the time. It had all seemed so far away.

There had been a lot of Elder lessons, in those first days after Sam arrived. Deen had told her about how she should sing the alphabet song while her Care brushed her teeth. And he'd shown her how tree sap could close a small cut or scratch and stop the bleeding. "Little kids *hate* bleeding," he'd said. She was glad she remembered those things now, but what else? How much had she forgotten? She should have paid better attention.

Oh, Deen.

As Jinny tugged at the blue blanket, Ess turned over and muttered, "Mama?" Jinny winced as she climbed up into the bed. *Mama*. She wished she could wipe the memories of *that* particular word from Ess's mind right away. It would make the next few weeks so much easier.

Still, as Jinny lay in bed, rubbing her tongue against the itchy burned roof of her mouth, listening to the night rain begin to patter on the roof of her cabin, and hugging Deen's worn sleeping shift, which smelled so familiar, she couldn't help wondering what it felt like . . . to remember.

Silent, in the darkness, Jinny let a few tears come.

3

Explosion of Morning

Jinny woke early the next day because something was *in* her nose. At first she rolled over and tried to sniff away the bug, or whatever it was. When the bug didn't fly off, Jinny opened her eyes, reached to swat at her face, and discovered that the bug was not a bug but a finger.

"Ugh!" she shouted, slapping the small hand away and sitting up in bed. "What are you *doing*, Ess?"

Ess scrambled back to the other end of the bed. Her eyes were now scared, but framed by a ridiculous lopsided tangle of hair. Jinny couldn't help wanting to laugh at her.

"Why did you do that?" asked Jinny, scrubbing her nose with the back of her hand.

The girl's big eyes started to fill with tears. She shook her head wordlessly, then pulled a blanket over herself.

"Oh, jeez," said Jinny, patting the lump under the blanket. "Never mind. It's fine. Just please don't cry. Please? Don't? Okay?" The crying continued to shudder the blanket, so Jinny reached for a shell on the windowsill and said, "Hey, I'll give you a present if you stop. Don't you want a present?" She held out the shell.

Ess stuck her head back out from under the blanket, gulped, and nodded at Jinny. Her fingers snatched the shell, but tears were still trickling down her face to her chin. Jinny watched the tears fall and darken the blanket, feeling helpless.

Then she had a thought. "Hey!" Jinny said, jumping down out of the bed and trying to sound cheerful and distracting. "Hey, I know. Are you hungry?"

The girl looked up at her, still crying but now also startled. She nodded again and whispered through a shudder, "Ess h—hungy."

Jinny clapped her hands together. "Good! I mean, not good, exactly, but I know how to fix *that*, at least. Let's get up and start the day. Nobody else will be up so early. It's still pretty dark out. Do you like eggs?"

Ess shrugged meekly, sniffing back tears.

"So okay, let's get moving!" Jinny turned her back to Ess and slipped as discreetly as she could out of her sleeping shift and into her tunic and pants, but when she turned back around to hang the sleeping shift on its hook, she found that Ess wasn't looking at her. Instead, the girl was deeply engaged in picking her nose. Jinny blanched at the sight but said nothing. She didn't want to start Ess weeping again, but she did wonder what an Elder was supposed to do about a habit like that. Deen hadn't given her any lessons at all on the nose-picking front. Jinny was sure she'd remember if he had. She tried not to cringe as the little girl slid down from the bed with one finger still in her nostril.

But when the two girls stepped out of the cabin onto the sandy path, the problem melted away. At the sight of the early morning, Ess was so awestruck, she withdrew the offending finger to raise both hands skyward in delight. "Ahh!" she gasped.

Directly overhead, the sky was a blue-purple color, stained with the last traces of night. Above the mist in the distance over the water, the sun was beginning to streak and shine, sending golden snakes writhing out into the rich expanse of the sky and waking up the day.

"Yeah?" said Jinny, glad to see the sudden change in the girl's mood. "See, I told you sunrise shapes are best of all. But wait. Just wait a minute. This is only the beginning. We're in time for everything. Hang on. . . ."

Ess watched the sky with an unblinking gaze. The girl's eyes widened when the sky began to lighten, as the snakes continued to make their way into the morning, fingers of fire carving up the lavender expanse and setting pictures in motion. Blazing wheels and tumbleweeds began to turn. They burst into vines, which rippled overhead, sprouting buds. Ess gasped, her mouth open wide, but when the buds blossomed into petals of fire, she screamed and clapped her hands, and Jinny couldn't help laughing with her. No matter how many times she saw it, the explosion of morning was breathtaking. In the end, the flowers became a field of glittering dust, a school of flitting fish, stars and particles of light that faded, vanished into day.

Then the sun was fully up and the sky was a perfect blue, pale and calm, a mirror reflection of the sea below. Now it was morning, and the birds were awake and calling to one another over the lapping surf on the beach. Ess grinned happily, flashing tiny white teeth.

Jinny grinned back. She hadn't really seen Ess smile yet. It was a relief to know she could. Maybe it wouldn't be so hard, having a Care.

"You don't have that kind of sunrise where you come from, huh?" Jinny asked, reaching over to pat down a tuft of curls that was sticking straight up from the girl's head.

Ess shook her head emphatically.

"Yeah, it's like that every day. Or anyway, it's just a little different every day. I don't know why that happens, or how. But isn't it terrific?"

Ess bounced lightly on her toes. "Ess," she lisped.

"Okay, come on," said Jinny. "I'll show you everything.

Let's get moving. I don't even know where to start. I guess right here?" She stretched out an arm and motioned at the line of eight weathered wooden buildings. "These are our sleeping cabins. They're all alike, pretty much."

The sleeping cabins sat on the curved sandy path that ran along the ridge above the dunes that fringed the beach. Each with a single window, like an unblinking eye, gazing out to sea. The grass surrounding the cabins was short and prickly, and pale pink crabs skittered at their feet, each the size of a fingertip. When she noticed them, Ess dropped to the sand.

"Dis?" she asked, pointing. "Whah *dis*?"

"Those are scuttles," Jinny explained. "They don't bite or pinch. But they'll come into your cabin when it gets really hot out. Then you have to sweep them out with a broom, or you'll step on them in the night, when you aren't looking, and *that* hurts." Ess didn't seem to be listening very well. She was busy trying to set a scuttle on her nose. The scuttle didn't want to sit.

"When I was about your age, Deen tried to drop one of those down my tunic." Jinny smiled at the memory. "So I popped him good on the nose, and he never tried *that* again. Sometimes, you just have to pop people. You know?"

Ess stared up at her very seriously, as if considering this important lesson, and Jinny found herself thinking that this probably wasn't the sort of advice Elders were supposed to pass on. Even if it was true.

"Okay then, moving on," she said, looking up at the three small buildings on the next ridge, just uphill from the sleeping cabins. She could show Ess the storehouse and book cabin later, but she figured the girl might need the wishing cabin right away. "Come on," she said, pointing. "Next I'll show you where to wish."

"Wiss?" Ess looked confused.

"Over here," said Jinny. She hiked up the path, opened the cabin door, and pointed to a basket on the floor that sat beside the wooden box that was the wishing hole. "Those leaves are for wiping. And if you take the second-to-last one, you need to gather more. I'll show you where to pick them. There's only one kind we use for this, and you don't want to make a mistake about that, trust me."

Ess didn't reply, but she nodded and reached immediately for the knob.

Jinny had a thought. "You don't . . . erm . . . need my *help*, do you? With wishing?"

Ess turned back to look at Jinny, shook her head in a proud way, and then trotted into the dark cabin and closed the door behind her.

"I guess you had to go," muttered Jinny. She felt relieved at the realization that there were some things Ess could do for herself.

When Ess had finished, Jinny took a quick turn herself. Then the two girls ran back down along the path, past the sleeping cabins and over the dunes to the beach below. As they made their way, Jinny pointed out the fishing nets and crab pots that hung off the side of the tiny dock in the cove, and the outdoor kitchen in the center of the camp, with its metal roof that overhung the cookstove, food safe, sink, and cupboards, as well as a large block of wood used for chopping. Just beyond the overhang of the roof were the long wooden dinner table and benches, the well, and the fire circle. Both girls took a minute to splash warm water on their hands and faces from the kettle, which had been sitting on the fading cookstove embers all night.

Watching the little girl wash up, Jinny couldn't help thinking about how absolutely new she was to all this. Jinny would have to show her everything—the beach that stretched on forever, wrapping around to the other side of the island. There were tide pools over there, full of bright petalfish, the watery flower creatures that shrank when they were touched. In the shallow water beyond the rocks there were sea stars too, a field of their strange bumpy bodies. Jinny would take Ess up the dunes and into the lush green center of the island, full of fruit trees, berry bushes, chickens, and the stream. She'd introduce her to the prairie, with its high grasses, beehives, and the colony of cats nobody could seem to gentle. And she'd take her up through the boulders to the cliffs, where the winds rushed. It was nice there. Ess could look out over the sea from above, watch the birds nest in the rocks.

That had been Deen's favorite thing of all. To watch the seabirds. "I wonder where they go," he used to say. And then the two of them would try to imagine it. . . .

Deen.

She shook her head, as if she could clear it that way, fling off the unwanted thoughts—the fact that he wouldn't be at breakfast, cracking nuts for Sam to eat, and he wouldn't be around to walk with her later and collect driftwood for the fire. He wouldn't be anywhere. Never again. He was out *there* now, wherever *there* was. Away.

Maybe where the seabirds went.

4

Having a Care

Jinny started for the metal food safe in the outdoor kitchen. "Come on, Ess," she called briskly over her shoulder. "There's got to be something left to eat from yesterday's fetch."

Ess followed eagerly, and it turned out they were in luck. Right away, Jinny found some chicken eggs in the bottom of the wire basket, and a few ripe plomms too. Normally, Ben was in charge of the cooking, as Joon was in charge of the fire, and Oz and Jak handled the fishing. But Jinny could roast an egg on her own. She sliced the soft, fuzzy plomms into quarters on the big wooden chopping block. She built the cook fire back up with dried dune grass, then added fresh wood in a rough pyramid shape. Once the stove was roaring, she set the eggs and wedges of fruit on top, and sat to wait.

Ess watched all this with huge eyes that followed Jinny everywhere. She missed nothing. When Jinny leaned over to poke at the fruit and make sure nothing burned, Ess leaned beside her and asked. "What dis?"

"What's what?" said Jinny.

The girl pointed to the plomms. "What d*is*?"

"Oh. Those are plomms."

Ess's forehead wrinkled, staring at the large, red, fuzzy fruits. "Bomms?"

"Plomms. They're good. They're like—I don't know. Plomms are like plomms. They're sweet and soft on the inside, and fuzzy outside. You'll love them. I promise. They grow on trees up past the prairie. I'll show you later. Didn't you have plomms? Where you came from?"

Ess shook her head.

Then Jinny had a thought. "Hey, what's it *like*," she asked, "where you came from?"

Ess shrugged and then stretched her arms up as tall as they would go. "Big!" she said. But before she could add anything more, there was a crazy loud pop from the stove, and Ess screamed and covered her head.

Jinny leaped up too, shouting. "Oh! *Oh!* My fault! I forgot to prick the eggs. Watch out. Get down. Now!"

Whizzzz. Pop! Pow! All the eggs were exploding. Jinny and Ess dropped to the sand and put their arms over their faces until the bits of shell stopped blistering the air around them.

When Jinny looked up again, Ben was standing beside her, laughing, still in his sleeping shift. "What made you think *you* could make breakfast, Jinny?" he asked.

All around her, the other kids stood in a circle now, grinning. Even Sam, who trailed behind the others, wore a quiet smile, though his eyes were red rimmed.

Only Eevie didn't smile. "Thanks a lot, *Jinny*. You woke us up." Her quick fingers darted in and out, braiding the long hair that draped over one shoulder. Eevie was particular about her hair.

Jinny ignored her. "Ess was hungry," she said to Ben.

"Ess?" asked Oz, grinning. "*That's* her name? Ess?"

"Yeah, Ess," answered Jinny. "What's so funny about Ess, *Oz*?"

Oz laughed. "Nothing, I guess!" He leaned over and stuck out a hand to shake. "Welcome to the island, Ess!"

Beside Oz, Jak stuck out his hand too. "Welcome, Ess," he echoed. This was no surprise. Jak generally did whatever Oz did, ten seconds behind the older boy. They were two boats apart in age but otherwise nearly identical.

Ess stared at the hands stuck out in front of her face. She didn't seem to know what to do with them. She waited, confused. After a moment, she decided to stick out her own little hand alongside the other two, as though *this* was the way people greeted each other on the island. Hand extended, she looked up at the boys for approval. They grinned, and Jinny tried not to laugh. "Ess," she said, "this is everyone. Everyone, this is Ess."

Ess looked around cautiously. She didn't say anything, but she seemed interested in the faces smiling down at her.

"That's Sam," said Jinny, pointing. "He's just a year older than you. Isn't that nice? Just one boat. You guys can play together!" Ess nodded hesitantly as Jinny continued. "Then, let's see . . . next in line is Nat, with the very short hair. She's quiet, kind of like you. And supersmart." Nat gave a gentle wave and smiled at Ess. Ess couldn't help smiling back. It was hard not to smile at Nat.

"After that," said Jinny, "is Jak, who you already met, with the ripped pants, *as usual*." Jak laughed. "And then Eevie is beside him. I'm sure she plans to be decent today, right Eevie?"

Eevie rolled her eyes skyward. "I'm always decent."

"Then Oz comes next. He's a bigger version of Jak, as you can see, and even louder." Oz snorted when she said that. "Joon is over there. She knows how to do everything *fast*." Joon waved. "And Ben is next in line. He's helpful. If you ever need something and I'm not around, ask Ben. He's the Elder-in-training now, right, Ben?" Ben nodded. "Then there's me, last of all. Because I'm oldest. That's all of us. Got it?"

Ess didn't answer Jinny, just peered around slowly, studying the huddle of interested faces. Of course she didn't get it all, thought Jinny. There was too much to get. But she was trying.

Ben smiled. "Now that you've met everyone, Ess, how would you like some *real* breakfast?"

Ess nodded again with a shy smile. "Ess," she whispered.

"Good!" said Ben, turning to the fire.

"Hey, don't I get credit for trying, at least?" Jinny asked Ben. "I made eggs, didn't I?"

Ben laughed. "You made a mess, is what you made. Now, get to work, Jinny. We need more firewood. Go."

"Hey!" said Jinny. "You don't get to tell me what to do. I'm the Elder, remember?"

"*Gosh,* she's going to be just unbearable now, isn't she?" said Eevie to nobody in particular. Jinny ignored the comment.

"Even so," said Ben, "I don't think anyone wants you in charge of the kitchen, Jinny." The others laughed, and he shouted pleasantly, "All of you, get to your chores, or I'm not cooking!"

Like clockwork, everyone ran to their morning tasks. Nat and Eevie set the long wooden table with pewter plates and cups, forks and spoons. Oz and Jak headed loudly to the well to haul up a pitcher of cold water. And long-legged Joon ran off on an emergency fetch, to get replacement eggs from the chickens.

Jinny tried to nudge Ess off somewhere so that she could do her firewood duty without the tiny girl slowing her down. She pointed to where Sam was helping to sweep the scuttles out from under the dining table with a twig broom. Unfortunately, Ess wasn't interested in sweeping, or Sam. She insisted on following close behind Jinny. As she moved along the beach, Jinny couldn't help noticing what a funny run Ess had. She was so thin, it was almost like her body couldn't quite hold up her big head, like she wasn't balanced quite right. Ess ran like she was throwing herself forward, arms flailing. She tipped over a *lot*. It was hard not to smile, watching her tilt.

When they were all gathered again by the fire, Ben scrambled some eggs and picked a few choice sprigs from the herb garden. In no time, the nine children were eating a fine omelet and the sweet roasted plomms. Using both hands, Ess gobbled up every bite. "Umm."

"Ugh, Cares!" exclaimed Eevie, watching Ess lick her fingertips. "Can't she even use a spoon yet?"

Jinny glared across the table. "Ess can eat any way she pleases, and it's none of your concern. Got it? Besides, you were a Care yourself, just a few years back."

Eevie stuck out her tongue in reply and added, "They were long years, and I'm naturally neat. Anyway, you're not the boss of everyone, Jinny. It doesn't have to be your way all the time, you know."

Jinny managed not to respond.

At the end of breakfast, when Eevie reached out to snatch the last plomm from the platter, Oz shouted, "Hey, no way!" and slapped at her hand. Then he grabbed the piece of fruit and jammed it in his mouth before anyone had a chance at it.

"Hey!" said Eevie. "I had it first!"

"You already had three," said Oz, talking through a visible mouthful of chewed fruit.

"Ugh!" said Eevie. "You're terrible. And I did *not* have three. I had two!"

"Oh, well then," said Oz, pretending to pull the half-chewed fruit from his mouth. "You want this one back?"

Eevie shot him a disgusted look. "You're a disaster. As usual."

"Am I? Am I really?" Oz asked. "Well then, I should clean myself up." He leaned over to wipe his chin on her shoulder.

"Ugh, Oz!" shouted Eevie, shoving him with an elbow. But when she did, it was Ess, not Oz, who toppled off the bench.

"Hey!" called Ben from the other end of the table, rising slightly so he could see better. "What just happened? Where's the new girl?"

Jinny peered under the table, to where Ess was sitting in a ball, her thin arms wrapped around her legs. "You okay?" Jinny whispered.

Ess nodded but didn't move.

Jinny sighed and called out, "She's okay, I think." Then she peered back down at Ess again. "They're just being goofs," she whispered. "But you stay down here as long as you want. Okay?"

Ess nodded again, but she still looked worried. Jinny wasn't sure what to do at first, but then she had an idea. "You know what?" she said. "How about if I join you?" She slipped under the table herself and scooched across to sit beside Ess. Jinny had to hunch, cramped, her head tilted sideways beneath the wooden planks. "Well, hi," she whispered at Ess. "Fancy meeting *you* here." She reached out and gave the girl a poke in the ribs.

With her head at such a funny angle, Jinny couldn't see very well, but she could hear it when Ess began to laugh. A breathy, uncontrollable sound. *Heh-heh-heh*.

Jinny glanced around as best she could, at all the legs, the dirty bare feet of different sizes, hanging off the benches on either side of the table. It was familiar, this sight, safe. She couldn't recall the last time she'd done this, but a memory welled up in her. A physical sensation of what it had been like to be little. It had been nice. So why did she feel sad, remembering?

"I think this is going to be nice—you and me," Jinny whispered. She couldn't keep the ragged edge from her voice when she added, "Don't you think so too?" Jinny reached out and squeezed the girl's knee.

"Ess!" came the small but cheerful reply. Then a hand found Jinny's and patted it, as if Ess was the one cheering her, and not the other way around.

5

Lose Your Shoes

After breakfast was over and the plates had been scrubbed with sand and rinsed with warm water in the big metal tub that served as a sink, Jinny waved good-bye to the others and pulled Ess off down the beach—not as far around the island as the tide pools, but still a long way. The two girls walked until they couldn't see the cove anymore, or the camp and cabins, to where a dead tree stuck up out of the sand, smooth and white like a bone. At the base of the tree was a huge sandy mound. There, Jinny stopped walking.

"What dis?" asked Ess, poking the mound with a finger. She squinted up at Jinny, curious.

"This is where you lose your shoes," Jinny said.

"Sooze?" said Ess.

"Yep, shoes," said Jinny, pointing at the girl's feet. "I'm not sure why, but we all do it. It's like an initiation. We put our shoes here when we first arrive. It's the way it's always been, since the beginning of the island, I guess. You give up your shoes, and then your feet will get nice and tough and strong like mine, and you'll be able to walk anywhere. Even on the rocks. Even in the tide pools—and they're sharp!"

Ess leaned over and touched the tips of her shoes. "Sooze. *Ess* sooze," she insisted.

"Has to be done," said Jinny with a quick shake of her head. "Come on now." She leaned over to tug at the laces of the wet, sandy cloth shoes, but Ess gave a cry. "No sooze. Ess sooze. *Mama* sooze."

Jinny stood back and stared at the girl. She wasn't sure what to do. She'd never heard of a kid not wanting to give up her shoes before. Deen certainly hadn't mentioned Sam doing it. What was she supposed to do now? Should she grab the kid and just yank them off her feet? That didn't sound very nice. Or should she let her keep them? Did it really matter if Ess kept her shoes? What difference could it possibly make?

Then it was as if Deen swam into Jinny's head for a moment, reminding her in his new deep voice about the rules. Jinny thought of Tate and the curlyferns. She knew this was how it was supposed to happen, how it had always been done. She decided she didn't want to start right off the first day, breaking the rules.

If Deen was right, there was a reason for everything—a reason for the shoes, for why the littles were never allowed to bank the fire, for why they didn't try eating scuttles, a reason why nobody slept on the beach at night. Jinny couldn't think what most of the reasons were, but she knew the rules and remembered them, usually. At the very least, it was her job to teach the rules to Ess.

Jinny got down on her knees in the sand. "Look, Ess," she said, brushing at the pile of sand until she uncovered the very small shoes. "Look at them all. Mine are in here, and Sam's, and everyone's. See? It's neat, how they're all different. Some have laces, and some have buckles, and some are blue."

Ess nodded and pointed at her feet. "Ess sooze," she said, determined.

Jinny sighed. "It's a rule. Get it? We are *supposed* to do this, and then we get you new clothes. That's day one. Isn't that fun? New clothes! Don't you want new clothes?"

Ess thought about this for a moment, then nodded and added firmly, "But deeze *Ess* sooze."

Jinny sat in the sand. She stared at a tiny shoe on top of the pile. It had a little tarnished buckle on a strap. They'd once been black leather, she supposed. Now they were gray and stiff with salt and sand.

"How about this?" she said at last. "You can keep your shoe*strings*, but we'll put the shoes in the pile. How's *that*? If you get to keep *something*?"

Ess tilted her head to one side and frowned, like she was considering.

"And we'll tie the shoestrings into a bracelet, a pretty bracelet, and you can wear it on your arm. Okay? You can add shells to it, or stick flowers in. It'll be fun."

Ess held out her bare wrist and stared at it. At last she looked back at Jinny. Her brow was furrowed. She wasn't happy.

"Oh, come on, Ess!" said Jinny. "Pretty please? I don't want to sit here all day. I'll make you the best bracelet ever. Will you do it?"

The little girl stared at her doubtfully. Then at last she opened her mouth. "Ess," she said, nodding slowly.

"Thank goodness!" Quickly, before Ess could change her mind, Jinny reached down and unlaced the girl's shoes, twisted the strings together and began to knot them firmly around the skinny arm, doubled them over several times, into a thick cuff. "When I was your age," she said as she worked, "I *loved* bracelets. And necklaces. And rings. Trinkets of any kind, really. I don't know why, but they always made me feel happy." She stepped back to examine her handiwork. "Okay!" she said. "What do you think? Pretty good?"

Ess petted the grubby band, then turned her big eyes up at Jinny and smiled. "Pitty!" she said. "Pitty *and* doohd."

Jinny grinned. "Yes, pretty *and* good. *And* now can we put the shoes in the pile?"

Ess delicately set both her shoes on the very top of the pile, then stood a moment, staring at her arm. "Mama," she said, patting the bracelet again. A moment later, with no warning at all, she turned around and careened back down the beach in the direction of camp.

"Yikes," said Jinny, repiling the fallen shoes as best she could before briskly taking off after Ess. "Wait up!"

As she sprinted behind the girl, Jinny wondered if this was always how it was going to be. How had she never noticed before how much effort it was, having a Care? Faintly, she remembered the time Sam had tried to catch a kitten in the prairie, and how Deen, not Sam, had been the one to come home all scratched up. There had been a scrape right on the end of Deen's nose, she remembered, that caused him to go cross-eyed each time he tried to look down at it.

When she caught up with Ess, Jinny grabbed her hand. "Come on," she said. "This way! I want to show you something else!" She tugged Ess up over the dunes, onto a pile of low flat rocks that baked all day in the sun. This was where the island snakes spent their mornings, rolling their tight, smooth bodies in the warmth and hissing pleasantly.

"Oh!" cried Ess, freezing like a statue when she saw them. Hundreds of snakes, coiled and twitching on the smooth pale rocks.

Jinny crouched down beside her and pointed. "See?" she whispered, watching for the girl's response. "Aren't they something?"

"Pitty . . . ," breathed Ess, her mouth hanging slightly open. Then she glanced up at Jinny. "Ouch?" she asked.

"Ouch?" Jinny didn't understand at first. But then she got it and shook her head. "Oh, no! No, the snakes would never bite you. Our snakes aren't like the snakes in storybooks. Real snakes are safe. *Here*, anyway. . . ."

"Ohhh," said Ess. "Otay." She crouched down to stare.

The patterns on the snakes' skins were perfect, repeating endlessly in coils and stripes and ovals and diamonds, in all the colors of the island. The deep red of plomms and the pale sand color of the beach itself, the black of the night sky and the green of the prairie. Oz and Jak liked to come hunting the snakeskins to decorate their cabins, though the colors were never the same once the skins had been shed. The snakes took their colors with them.

After a few moments of watching, Ess unfroze and reached down to stroke one of the tight striped backs with two soft fingertips. She chose the smallest snake, and there was something sweet, Jinny thought, in how careful the girl was with the creature. For all her careening and jangling, Ess knew to be gentle and still with the fragile thing. She stroked its back, then looked up at Jinny like she'd seen something magical.

There *was* something magical about them, Jinny thought, watching. When one snake twitched, the others twitched too, as though they were all part of a piece of cloth, ripples in the same stretch of sea.

After that, Jinny led Ess home. Only instead of heading back for the long walk around the beach, the two girls took a shortcut, up the sandy path behind the dunes that led over the ridge. "Eech, eech ooch," cried Ess, letting out a sharp sound each time she stepped on a pebble, a shell, or a shorn bit of dried grass in her path. At one place she stopped, looked up at Jinny, and said with a sigh, "See. Ess *sooze*. . . ."

So Jinny took pity on the girl's tender feet and, with a groan, hefted her up onto a hip, to carry her the remainder of the hike, uphill at a steady pace. In no time at all they came around a clump of tangled bushes and found themselves in the place where the storehouse peered down at the sleeping cabins below. "Ooof," Jinny grunted as she set the girl down.

"Ooof!" repeated Ess, for no particular reason. She giggled, as though it was a good joke.

Jinny only rolled her eyes and reached to open the storehouse door with her left hand, while she waved her right hand in the air overhead, scattering moths and a spiderweb from the doorframe. This was the cabin used least frequently by the kids. Often they went sleeps and sleeps without entering this place. The hinges squeaked when the door swung open at Jinny's touch. Ess hung back at first, but Jinny pulled her inside.

In the dim room, lit by two dusty windows, shelves lined the walls, and on those shelves were all the things a person might need on an island. There were stacks of garments—folded tunics and pants, sleeping shifts and wraps for the occasional cool evenings—all of them cut from the same soft gray-green cloth. Beside the clothes sat extra blankets, blue, but worn with use.

On the floor beside the door, Ess found a box with old kitchen tools that had become rusty and been retired. But on the island, everything was saved. Even if something had been deemed useless, there was no good place to throw it, except perhaps down the wishing hole. Besides, even an old ladle with a broken handle might be used later for scooping ashes from the fire or digging up cattail roots on a fetch. Everything had its purpose. If you waited long enough, a useless thing would become useful again.

Jinny surveyed the stacks of clothing, picking out a sleeping shift and a day tunic for Ess, in the very smallest size, and also a pair of loose pants, which she handed to the younger girl. The kids wore these clothes until they fell to bits, and then the bits were washed and returned to the cabin, for the ragbag. Rags were used for all sorts of things, from games of blindman's bluff to bandaging small cuts.

Since she happened to be there anyway, Jinny decided to swap her own pants for a fresh pair, as they'd been getting threadbare. But when Jinny turned back around in her new pants, Ess was standing before her, completely naked in the middle of the dim room. She'd managed to unsnap her dress and drop it on the floor. Now she was waiting patiently for Jinny to help her with her new things.

"Oh!" said Jinny, blushing and turning away. She was used to seeing other kids in states of undress, but it still seemed funny. Ess was so very new, and so very naked.

Deen had warned Jinny that this might happen. Apparently Sam had done the very same thing. "Don't make your Care feel embarrassed," he'd said. "It'll be hard, but try not to laugh at her. Instead, *smile*. There's a big difference between smiling at someone and laughing at them."

Remembering, Jinny smiled now, and it worked! Ess smiled back.

"Dinny hep?" asked the girl. "Peeze hep?"

"Umm, yeah, sure, of course," said Jinny. She took the tunic and dropped the folds of cloth quickly over Ess's head. Then she wriggled the cloth down and around, until two thin arms found their way into the wide sleeves. When that was done, Jinny squatted down and, holding each tiny ankle, guided the wobbling girl into her pants.

As Jinny finished tying the drawstring on the pants and stepped back from her Care, Ess grinned and spun around, looking down at her new clothes. Like all the other kids, she now wore a tunic that fell to midthigh, with voluminous pockets, for when she went on a fetch. She looked very proud of herself. "Ess dess," she said, beaming and shoving her hands deep into the pockets.

"Yes, it's all yours," said Jinny, picking up Ess's old blue dress from home. "And now *this*," she said, "goes in the ragbag. But you'll still have your bracelet, okay? And you can keep it forever." She worried that Ess would be upset at losing the blue dress, but the girl appeared to be fine. Trading in her dress was somehow different from burying her shoes in a heap of sand and walking away.

After that was all done, Jinny opened the door to the storehouse, and the two girls walked out into the sunlit day. Together they trooped back down the path, past the sleeping cabins, to the beach, where Eevie and Nat were at work in the kitchen, shucking ersters.

"Jinny!" called Eevie, exasperated. "You've been gone all morning. You need to help us!"

"Let it go, Eevie," said Nat gently. "Jinny has a big job right now, getting used to being Elder."

"Thanks for understanding, *Nat.*" Jinny glared at Eevie. To Ess she added, "Don't mind her. She's always a little grouchy. I don't know why. She just came that way."

Ess nodded at this, though Jinny couldn't tell if she really understood. But the little girl slipped her hand nervously into Jinny's as they made their way over to the table.

"Well," Jinny said to Eevie, "if you want my help like you say, move over." She gave a gentle shove with her elbow and reached for a knife. "And get your hair out of the way. Jeez! I don't want to sit on it." Eevie whipped her long tight braid sharply away.

Meanwhile, Nat tossed shells into a basket. "Anyway, we're

nearly done," she said. "Maybe we should all go for a swim, wash off before lunch?" Everyone nodded and shucked a little faster.

Ess watched the three older girls at work on the ersters. Their hands moved so quickly, picking up and dropping the shells. She stared at the knives flashing. "Wha dis?" She pointed after a bit.

"Oh!" said Nat in a soft voice. "Ersters? You don't know ersters?"

Ess shook her head.

"I know they don't look like much," added Nat, "all goopy and slimy, but they'll make you strong. Here, try one." She held out the half shell full of gelatinous glop.

Everyone stopped shucking for a moment, to watch as Ess stuck out her pointy pink tongue and touched the erster with it tentatively. Then she wrinkled her nose and looked up at Jinny. "Dinny like dis?" she asked.

"We all do," said Jinny, nodding.

Nat added, "And *you* will soon enough, I bet. But maybe you'll try one grilled first. How would that be?" She passed the offending erster to Eevie, who leaned down to slurp it up and then gasped. "Hey, look!"

"Wha?" asked Ess, standing up to see what Eevie had found. When she did, she gasped too. Inside the shell, something gleamed. Ess poked at it. "Wha *dat?*"

"It's a moonball, Ess," said Nat. "I'm not sure how, or why, but that pretty pink moonball *grows* in there, inside that ugly erster. Isn't that funny?"

Ess looked mesmerized by the moonball. Her hand hovered over the shell, tentative, as though she wanted to snatch it up. But before she could make up her mind to touch it, Eevie's hand shot out and plucked it for herself. "And it's *mine*!" she crowed, holding it up in the sunlight.

Ess looked crestfallen.

"Oh, Eevie," said Nat. "We should share with her. It's her first one, and she's little. Who knows when we'll find another. Especially a pink one."

Eevie shook her head. "She's not *that* little. And nobody ever gave *me* a moonball. Humph."

Jinny frowned at Eevie, then stood up and reached out a hand to her Care. "Come on, Ess. Enough ersters and cranky meanies. Let's find something else to do."

"Sorry, Ess!" called Nat, as they walked away.

6

Bedtime Tales

That evening, when Jinny and Ess arrived and offered to help with dinner, Ben looked surprised. "Wow," he said softly. "You did the shoe thing already . . . and got her clothes?"

"Sure," said Jinny. "That's day one, isn't it? Shoes and clothes?"

"I guess so," said Ben, turning away to mix something in a bowl. "I just . . . I thought I was supposed to go too. For my Elder lesson."

"Oh," said Jinny. "Well, sorry, but no. Deen didn't even take *me* along for that. Anyway, it's hardly something you need a lesson for. You take off the shoes. You put them on the pile. You change clothes and put the old ones in the ragbag. Easy peasy."

"O-okay," said Ben. "I guess I can do that."

"Well, of course you can," scoffed Jinny. "Anyone can." Then she turned to Ess. "Let's help set the table, okay?" And together, they all laid out the plates and cups, as Ben served up a good dinner of dandelion salad and grilled ersters, which it turned out Ess *did* prefer to raw.

After dinner, all nine kids gathered around the fire. Suddenly, Jinny had a flash of memory, recalled this same night, exactly one year prior. Deen had taken his usual spot beside her, but on his other side, for the first time, Sam sat, quietly nervous. Chewing his fingers.

"I feel funny," Deen had whispered to Jinny. "It feels strange, without Tate. I don't remember what to do."

"You'll be great," she'd promised him. "I know it."

Then Deen had taken a deep breath, put an arm around Sam, and said . . .

"Oh!" Jinny cried, suddenly remembering and turning to Ess. "I know what I'm supposed to tell you now! About the stars!"

"Tars?"

"Yes," said Jinny. "See, this is what we do, every single night—we gather around the fire, just like this. But now look, up there, see?" She pointed at the sky and whispered, as the others settled into their places. "See how there are starting to be stars in the sky?"

Ess nodded.

"Well, you should always come here, to this very spot, when you see three stars in the sky. That's a *rule*—do you understand? Three stars? It's important. Everyone does this, just the same way. So if we can all see three stars, but we don't see you, we'll worry. Understand?"

Ess nodded solemnly.

Jinny stared at the eight faces surrounding her and felt sad and happy all at the same time. It seemed impossible that only two nights ago, Deen had been sitting in that same spot, with his knee touching Jinny's. Now there were three stars, but he was gone, and it was as though everything was somehow the same for the rest of them. Happy to enjoy dinner and the fire.

Jinny stared across the fire at Sam, seated now at Ben's knee. The boy was holding a stick and gazing off into space. She wondered what he was thinking. But not enough to call across to him.

"Hey, aren't you going to read, Jinny?" called out Joon.

"Oh! I didn't think . . . I forgot . . . to grab a book," said Jinny. It hadn't occurred to her that the nightly reading was her job now too, with Deen gone. "Should I run and get something?"

Around the fire, heads nodded in agreement, so Jinny hopped up and ran through the darkening night to the book cabin, a path her feet knew by heart. It didn't matter what she grabbed. With the exception of Ess, they'd all read just about every book in the place. She reached blindly.

Back at the fire circle, Jinny opened the book, cradling its worn spine in one hand as she turned the soft, crumbling pages with the other. All the kids knew to be careful with the books. They were swollen, faded, eaten by the salt air and the grit of sand, not to mention so many grubby, grabbing fingers. When a book died, there was nothing to be done about it. The kids could only bury it in the sandy earth beyond the book cabin door and try to remember the story. They marked these little graves with the biggest shells they could find. It made a funny sort of garden.

Jinny wondered, whenever she walked between the carefully placed shells, what books there had been before she came to the island. What stories were planted in the ground that had died before she got there. Books she'd never know, their pictures disintegrating in the earth, their characters gone forever. It was a funny thought, strange to imagine the bright stories in the dark ground, surrounded by scuttles and bugs.

Jinny cleared her throat and looked up at the other kids who ringed the fire, their faces flickering in the flames, with their foreheads hot and their backs cold against the breezy night. They talked quietly to each other, and nobody seemed to be paying especially close attention to her but Ess, so Jinny said, "Hey, I know you've all heard this before, but if you want me to read, you need to listen."

Across the fire, Oz gave a grumble. Jak grumbled too, but

Ben said, "Shhhh," and everyone fell silent.

It was hard for Jinny to make out the words in the uneven light, but she could almost recite this story from memory anyway. "'Once there was a tree . . .'"

Beside her, Ess listened, mouth hanging slightly open, to the tale of a tree that gave everything it had to a boy—its apples and its branches, until the tree was nothing but a stump. It was a sad story, Jinny thought, but what a thing to do—to give up your whole self for someone else. To love someone that much. To be always and forever *there*, no matter what. To hold on like that.

When she was finished, Sam piped up suddenly, from across the fire circle. "I wish *our* trees would talk to me," he said wistfully.

"That'd be nice, wouldn't it," said Ben, with a smile for the smaller boy.

"Not me," said Joon, shaking her head. "Imagine if you went out to wish in the middle of the night and some tree was like, 'A little too much tea before bed tonight, huh?'"

Everyone laughed at that.

"Well, I think the tree is stupid," said Eevie.

Jinny rolled her eyes in the darkness.

"Hey, Jinny," called out Nat. "What did Abigail think of this one? I can't remember what she wrote."

"Oh, good question," said Jinny. She flipped to the front of the book and peered at the handwriting inside the cover. It was hard to make out the faint scribbles in the flickering light of the fire. She squinted. "Hmm. Actually, Abigail seems to agree with Eevie on this one. She wrote, 'That tree is a pathetic doormat. It got what it deserved.'"

Across the fire, Eevie looked triumphant. "*See*," she said. "Told you so."

"Well, since you know so much, Eevie, what's a doormat?" asked Oz.

Eevie snorted. "If you don't know, I'm not going to tell you," she said.

"Awww, you don't know," hooted Jak.

"Anyway, I'm going to bed," said Eevie, yawning. "It's late."

"Agreed," said Ben, standing up. "Come on, let's all head to bed. We might get caught in night rain if we don't go soon."

One by one, the kids rose from the fire circle and called out their good-nights as they filed up to the path and their cabins. But Jinny sat a moment, watching them go, because Ess was leaning heavily against her legs. It was only when Jinny moved to pick her up that she realized Ess was still wide awake, eyes staring at the bright stars overhead, the soft night all around her.

"Hey, you're still up," said Jinny. "What're you thinking about?"

The little girl looked at her with tired eyes and said quietly, "For Ess? All for Ess?"

"What?" Jinny didn't understand her question at first.

"Dis," said Ess, tossing a thin arm wide, to gesture at the sky, the fire, the other children walking back to their cabins in the moonlight. "All dis for Ess?"

"Oh," said Jinny. "Yeah." Then she whispered, "All for Ess."

All for Ess, thought Jinny, as she pulled her Care to standing and held her hand across the sand, guided her to the path that led up the hill to bed. All for Ess, this wonderful place, for years and years to come. Jinny sighed. How would she ever leave it all, when her turn came? How had Deen let go so easily?

Back in their cabin the two girls slipped into their sleeping shifts. Then they crawled into bed and settled down, tip to toe again, one head at each end of the bed. Tonight they did it easily, comfortably, as if they'd been sleeping this way forever.

As she nodded off to sleep, Ess called out a question in her thin voice. "Dinny?"

"Yes," said Jinny sleepily from the other end of the bed.

"Whooze . . . Abidal?"

At first Jinny was too drowsy to make sense of the slurry words, but then she understood. "Oh, *Abigail*! From the story, you mean? Abigail with the *pathetic doormat*?"

"Ess," said Ess.

"Abigail Ellis," said Jinny, yawning. "That was her name. She must have lived here a long time ago, or before I came anyway, and before anyone who was here when I arrived. We don't know much more about her than that, except she wrote her name in all the books and made notes in them. So we like to read what she had to say. It's almost like . . . almost like we know her. Like she's part of our family. Like she's part of the island. She's the only kid we know about from before we all got here. The only person who left a name behind."

"Oh," said Ess. "Otay."

Jinny propped herself up on her elbows and watched the girl sink into her pillow at the other end of the bed, watched her eyes close. She thought about how nice it would be to fall into a pillow exactly that way—to close your eyes and fall off to sleep with an answer. Just like that.

7

Almost Magical

The next morning, after Jinny and Ess had rolled out of bed, Ess ran to open the cabin door, but Jinny had a thought. "Hey now!" she called out. "It's time you learned to straighten up after yourself. You need to help me make this bed. After all, you slept in it too! Get over here!"

Ess looked surprised, but she flashed a quick smile. "I do! I hep!" she said eagerly, reaching for the covers, which she promptly dragged straight down onto the floor.

Jinny laughed and picked up the blankets. She showed Ess how to hold two corners of the sheet and blanket and shake them free of sand and dirt. She taught her to tuck the sheet neatly under the mattress. Watching Ess run her tiny hands around the bed, pulling and tucking at each pucker, made

Jinny smile. When that was done, the two of them plumped the pillows and pulled the blanket up over the bed, tucking it neatly under.

"Why dis?" asked Ess with a grunt, pushing hard to get the corner of the blanket securely under.

"Just so that we don't end up with scuttles or bugs in the bed," said Jinny, wrinkling her nose.

Ess wrinkled her own nose in imitation and grinned at Jinny. Then she said, "No. Why do dis?" gesturing at the entire bed. She patted a pillow gently and smoothed over the top of the blanket, which Jinny had turned neatly over.

"Oh, why do we make the bed?" asked Jinny. "I don't know. Because we do. Because that's the way of it. Because . . . it makes it nicer to come back into the cabin each night."

Ess responded with a soft nod.

And the next day, and the day after that, Ess scrambled down from the bed each morning and immediately began to tug at the blankets, squealing when they toppled over onto her head. She liked her task. She liked knowing exactly what she was supposed to do. It seemed to please her, to help.

Ess had been on the island for about ten sleeps, and settled into the pattern of life—meals at the long table with the others, naps in the late afternoon, stories by the fire circle—when one morning, Ben asked Jinny if she'd join Joon on a fetch. "We're almost out of fresh snaps, and you're the best picker of all of us. Plus, we should set a bunch of them out to dry. We haven't done that in a long time. Please?"

"Fine, but what should I do with Ess?" asked Jinny, swallowing a mouthful of cold fish. "She's not ready to climb the boulders yet."

"Sure she is," offered Joon. "She's got to learn, doesn't she?"

"She'll slow us down," said Jinny. "She could get hurt."

"So what if she does?" asked Joon. "Everyone gets hurt sometimes."

"I suppose," said Jinny. "But while I'm her Elder, it's my job to keep her safe. Isn't it?"

"Is it?" asked Ben. "I thought it was your job to teach her to keep *herself* safe. Otherwise, what happens when you go? Anyway, Sam did it last year, with Deen," said Ben. "Remember?"

"I guess so," grumbled Jinny. She was the Elder. Why did Ben always have to be so right?

An hour later, the three girls set off with large cloth sacks to hold the sweet fresh snaps. They hiked up past the cabins, through the wide green meadow to where the low snap trees stood, at the edge of the cliffs. Jinny was surprised to see that Ess was able to keep up with Joon's pace, scurrying along beside her, stumbling in her ungainly way, where Joon took long, even strides. Once, Ess slipped and fell, but she didn't cry, and she popped up right away and kept going.

From behind, Jinny couldn't help noticing that Joon and Ess resembled each other. She'd never noticed it before, but their coloring was the same—like the rich dark soil of the prairie. Their arms were long and thin. Both of them had the same wild, wonderful curls too. Jinny wondered if maybe, as she grew, Ess would shoot up tall and angular, like Joon. Sharp.

Of all the kids, Joon was the one who knew the island best. She was strong and long legged and loved to explore, to range and roam. Sometimes she even spent nights away from her cabin, roosting with the chickens in the trees, or camping out on the prairie. Jinny and Joon were only two boats apart in age, but somehow, though Jinny liked Joon, she never felt that she knew her entirely. Joon kept something to herself, always. As though she had a secret and would never tell it.

It was nice, picking in the cool late morning together. Ess stuffed her face with the sweet snaps, chewing their meaty red flesh and spitting out the pits. But she put as many into the bags as she did into her mouth, so Jinny didn't scold much. She only said, "You'll make yourself sick, you know." The low trees were just right for Ess's short arms to climb, and now and then she'd chase after one of the wild cats that crept over from the high grass of the prairie to watch them warily. Jinny had to admit Ben had been right. She was glad she'd brought the girl along.

After a few hours, all the bags were filled, and it was time to climb the cliffs. Joon groaned as she pulled one heavy sack up onto her back and then led the way, while Jinny, carrying the second sack, and Ess, "helping," followed her up into the rocky foothills and strange arrangements of boulders that covered the base of the cliffs on that part of the island. They moved slowly, hauling their heavy load of fruit, picking their way carefully over the boulders and then along the faint sandy path in the rock. Several times, Jinny had to stop and help Ess up, but the younger girl didn't complain once, and at last they made their way to where the cliffs flattened out into low stretches of gray rock. The wind rushed all around the cliffs there, creating a roaring, blustery sound that kept most birds and animals away. But from above, the sun beat down, and the rocks stayed hot all day. It was the perfect place for fruit to dry.

One by one Jinny and Joon set the dark green-skinned fruits out on the dry rocks. If they were lucky, and the birds didn't steal too many of them, the sunshine would shrink and sweeten the firm globes into rich bits of chewy deliciousness. In about a dozen sleeps, they'd come back and collect them again. These dried snaps were the closest thing the kids had to what Abigail's books called *candy*. Ben liked to keep them always on hand, but recently, they'd gotten off schedule and run out. It felt like a hundred sleeps since Jinny had tasted a dried snap.

As Joon and Jinny worked, Ess danced from rock to rock, hunting for shell shapes and feather patterns buried in the ancient stone. Jinny watched her poke around. "You were right," she said to Joon. "She can do it."

"I know she can," said Joon tersely. She kept at her work, laying out fruit hand over hand, only taking a moment to shoot Jinny a quick sidelong glance. "She can probably do just about anything."

"What's *that* supposed to mean?" said Jinny.

"Just that Ben is right. It's not your job to help her every second. It's your job to teach her to help herself."

"I know that," said Jinny, turning her back on Joon. "I don't need the two of you telling me. Anyway, just wait until you have a Care. You'll see it isn't so easy."

Joon didn't reply. Instead she stood and stretched herself tall, then shouted, "Hey, Ess, watch this!" as she took a running leap off the top of the high cliff and, for an instant, shone bright, silhouetted against the sun. It looked like Joon would fall, and Ess gasped. But a second later a soft push of wind brought her feet back to solid ground.

Ess looked up at Jinny. "Ess do too?"

Jinny laughed. "Sure, of course. The wind will always push you back to land. The cliffs won't let you fall. You're safe."

She watched as Ess proceeded to toss her little body off the cliffs and into the wind, watched the girl sprawl on the rock when the gusts brought her gently back down. But for some reason, Jinny wasn't in the mood to jump herself. This—cliff jumping—had been something Jinny had done most often with Deen, and it felt wrong, to ride the wind without him.

She remembered one day, just before he'd gone. It had been a while since they'd come up to the cliffs alone. He was always with Sam. But that day they'd walked up together, just the two of them. At the top, they'd played a game. They'd stood, hand in hand, and jumped at the same time into the wind. Whoever managed to get both feet back on the ground first won. That day, Jinny kept winning. Every time. After twelve turns, she'd let go of his hand and laughed at him. "Ha, you lose!" she'd shouted.

Deen had shot her a cool look and turned silently to head back down the cliffs.

"Hey, wait, what's wrong with you all of a sudden?" Jinny had asked him. "What's wrong?"

Deen had shaken his head. "Sorry. Nothing. I'm just in a . . . I'm not feeling so great."

"Then why did you invite me up here?" asked Jinny.

"I don't know," he said. "It just felt like we should do this today. One more time."

"What are you talking about?" Jinny had asked. "Deen . . . are you okay?"

But instead of answering, he'd suddenly turned, run, jumped, tossed himself back into the wind. Alone.

Jinny didn't try to join him. And a few days later, the boat had arrived.

Now, looking back, the memory hurt. Jinny wondered if he had known, that day, what was coming. And if so, how? She wondered, too, if the wind blew so strongly where he was now. She wondered if Deen thought of her when he felt it blow. These thoughts filled Jinny's head as she watched Ess toss her thin body off the cliffs. The girl hurled herself fearlessly into the breeze, her arms and legs outstretched, a huge grin on her face. Ess shouted with joy each time she tumbled back gently onto the baked stone.

When the sun was high in the sky and the bags of fruit had all been laid out, Jinny stood up and called, "Time to go, guys!"

"No, no, no. Ess wants more!" cried Ess.

Joon stood with her hands on her hips and laughed. "Stay much longer up here on these sunny rocks and you'll pass out from heatstroke. It's time to go. But I bet you'll like the next part almost as much."

Jinny nodded, brushing the sticky juice from her hands onto her pants. "Joon's right," she said. "We need to skedaddle. But don't worry, Ess. This is good too. Come on!"

Then all thoughts of fruit drying and Deen and who was right and who wasn't were forgotten as the three girls sat down on the fruit sacks. With a shout they shoved off and slid all the way down the slopes, down to the foothills and the boulders. Ess shouted with joy as she rode in Jinny's lap down the smooth stone, the wind rushing past them, her hair tickling

Jinny's nose. Below them, the blur of the meadow and the prairie stretched out like a green-gold sea. Rushing along, Jinny felt better. Clearer. There was something almost magical about moving so fast.

8

Minor Adjustments

After her wonderful day on the cliffs, Ess begged constantly to return. "Now we go?" she asked every few hours. "Pease?"

But Jinny shook her head each time. "You can't do your favorite thing every day, or it won't be special anymore."

"Pooh," said Ess with a pout.

"We'll go back to get the dried snaps in ten sleeps," explained Jinny. "I promise."

Then one day at breakfast, Nat and Eevie announced they were heading out for a honey fetch.

Ess turned to Jinny, eyes wide, and begged. "Ess go too?"

Jinny laughed and nodded. "Sure, why not," she said. "It's not quite as exciting as the cliffs, but you'll like the bees."

An hour later, the four girls hiked up the path into the high grass. In no time at all, they reached the prairie, where the wild cats and the chickens had free range and chased each other back and forth. Even as the four of them stepped into the high green and gold grasses, a small orange kitten was worrying a big old hen into a frenzy near a rotting stump.

"No!" shouted Ess, running at the kit. "No! Shoo, kitty!"

The kitten turned and hissed at Ess, who jumped into the air with a screech, and the cat raced off, back in the other direction. Eevie laughed, and Jinny couldn't help joining her. But Nat crouched down and asked, "You okay, Ess?"

Ess pouted and said, "I was helping."

"We know you were," said Nat. "But the thing to remember about the animals is that they do fine on their own. They do fine without us."

"But," said Ess, looking worried, "but . . . kitty would *hurt* ticken."

"Yup," said Eevie. "It's a hard life in the prairie for a *ticken* that can't fight back!"

"Hey, you two!" Jinny interrupted. "Hey, let's get a move on. I want honey! Last to the hives is a stinker!"

They all took off running without argument.

When they arrived at the first hive, Jinny showed Ess how to raise the lid carefully, so as not to pinch her fingers. Ess was bothered a bit by the bees at first, and ran around waving her arms in the air whenever one landed on her. But then

Nat explained, in her calm voice, about how the bees didn't want to sting. How they would only sting if something went very, very wrong, if they were scared or hurt. So Ess settled down and came to watch as Jinny pulled a frame from the hive, ignoring the bees that crawled and buzzed and settled on her skin, tickling.

Ess watched as each of the older girls pulled a frame and laid it flat on the clean sheet they'd spread on the ground. Each of them gently brushed the bees from her frame with a stick, and then when the bees were gone, they took turns with a small knife, cutting the rectangles of dripping honeycomb from the wooden frames. In no time at all the frames were back in the hive, and the sheet had been folded up, with each comb nestled cleanly inside. Then the folded rectangle of cloth went into Jinny's fetch bag, and they had to run home fast, so that Ben could put it all in the honey pot before it oozed through the sheet.

"Come on!" Jinny called to Ess, who was walking home more slowly than the others. "We don't want to lose you."

"Go slow," called Ess. "I go slow, for Fuzzy."

Jinny fell back to see what Ess was talking about, and she found the girl with a bee cupped in her hand. With a gentle finger, Ess was stroking the bee's back.

"Oh, for Pete's sake, Ess," shouted Eevie from farther ahead. "Let the bee go."

"Fuzzy wants to stay," said Ess with a sharp little nod. She looked up at Jinny and Nat, who stood just behind her.

"Fuzzy needs to fly home to her family," said Nat gently, reaching out to uncup Ess's hand. "Nobody's meant to go off alone, away from her family. Families stay together. This bee needs her family too."

Jinny watched, wishing she'd thought to say that. Nat had a way with Ess. She was so calm. And now Ess was letting the bee go and taking Nat's hand instead. Inside, Jinny felt a tiny burn, and it surprised her.

But the burn wasn't just about Nat and Ess. In Jinny's mind, there was a picture suddenly. Of a tiny green boat in the distance. Of a boy, shouting something she couldn't hear. "Sometimes, people do go off alone," she muttered to herself as she kicked through the grass, carrying her bag of honey, which was now beginning to ooze. "Sometimes people do leave their families."

Even though Jinny loved her time with Ess, she found it was hard work having a Care. Each night at the fire circle, she was so tired she could barely keep her eyes open long enough to read a story. She found it was generally more difficult showing Ess how to do a chore than it had ever been to just do it herself.

There were so many things it had never occurred to Jinny a kid had to learn, so many things Jinny felt she'd always simply known but that it turned out Ess needed to be taught, things Deen had neglected to point out in his Elder lessons—to fetch water from the well in the smallest bucket when the kettle ran dry, because Ess couldn't carry the big one when it was full. Or how to pick swinks, the green berries the kids ate every day, from the brambly bushes up above the cabins on the ridge, without getting pricked. Jinny taught Ess to set the table and scrub the dishes with wet sand. She taught her to dig for clams along the beach and to pluck the fish from the nets and the crabs from their traps without squealing. Jinny taught Ess to gather the eggs the chickens laid in the prairie without spooking the birds. "Respect the ladies," she told Ess, as the little girl stared up at a hen roosting in the low branch of a tree. "We owe them a lot."

Now and then, Jinny would find Ben lurking nearby, when she was teaching Ess something. "Go away," she told him. "Shoo. You're making me nervous, always looking over my shoulder, spying on me."

"I'm not spying," said Ben. "I'm trying to see how to do it, so that I can be ready, next year. You said you'd let me know when it was time for each lesson. But you never remember, so I'm not learning anything. I don't even know if we need to do the wiping, when they wish—"

"Ew!" shouted Jinny. "Ew, no, Ben. No. They wipe themselves. Anyway, Ess does."

Ben shrugged. "Well, *see*, how would I know that if you don't tell me?"

"Oh, Ben," Jinny groaned. "Because you'd figure it out. Every single moment is a lesson, don't you see? You'll be fine when the time comes. You're a natural Elder! It's all just common sense. There's nothing for you to learn, really."

"It would still be nice if you taught me, like you're supposed to," said Ben, looking hurt. "Deen taught you, didn't he?"

"Sure," said Jinny. "Some of it, anyway. But that was mostly just because Deen and I spent so much time together. I just happened to be there a lot. It wasn't extra work for him."

"I didn't know it was extra work, spending time with me," said Ben.

"You know that's not what I meant," said Jinny. "Jeez, Ben," and she punched him lightly on the arm. "Anyway, the boat was just here. It won't come again for a long, long time. Right?"

"Maybe," said Ben. "But you'll forget things once you've done them. Now is when the lessons happen, in the beginning. This is my chance to see how it's done."

"Well, here," said Jinny, grinning. "This is how it's done." And she turned Ess upside down in the sand until the girl burst out laughing. "When in doubt, make your Care laugh. Laughter is the best medicine. Deen told me that!"

All in all, Jinny felt like she was doing a pretty good job with Ess, but no matter how she tried, she couldn't seem to teach the girl to swim. Deen had told Jinny that swimming was the most important lesson of all. He'd explained to her that an Elder was only really *required* to teach a Care three things—to cook a meal, to swim like a fish, and to read a book. "I don't know why those three," he'd said. "That's just what Tate told me."

So that was something Jinny explained to Ben. "The three things we really need to survive. Or that's what Deen said Tate said. When I figure out how to do any of them, I'll be sure to teach you the trick," she added with a laugh.

But it wasn't entirely funny, because when it came to swimming, Ess absolutely refused to learn. Each day after lunch, Jinny waded into the cove with her Care, their tunics billowing in the water, the big pockets inflating like balloons. Ess was fine with that part—the wading, as long as Jinny was holding her firmly. She even laughed when the fish swam by and tickled her bare legs. But the moment Jinny tried to let go of her, Ess screamed like she was being pinched by a crab. She shrieked and clung to Jinny's leg or arm or neck, whatever part she could grab. "Noooooooooo," she'd moan. "Ess no, no, no, no like swimming."

"Look, Ess," Jinny tried to explain, as Ess clung to her neck, "I know you're scared, but you *have* to learn to swim."

"Why?" Ess wanted to know.

"Because," said Jinny.

"Why?"

"Because you have to," said Jinny.

"Why?" Ess begged again.

Somehow, Jinny managed not to shout, *Because you're driving me absolutely crazy!* Instead, she pointed at Sam, off swimming by himself in a circle. "Hey, look!" she said to Ess, and then called out, louder, "Sam, hey, Sam! Tell Ess how much fun it is to swim!"

Sam heard her and paddled over, an eager smile on his face. "Sure, it's easy," he said. "I'll help you, Ess."

"See, Sam can do it," Jinny said to Ess, "and he's just a little bit older than you. If Sam can do it, you can do it too."

"Otay. I do it." Ess nodded, looking very earnest.

Jinny felt hopeful as Sam paddled around the two of them, and Ess kick-kick-kicked in her arms. But a few minutes later, when Jinny tried to let Ess loose in the water, Ess shrieked as usual. So Jinny stomped back up onto the beach again, dragging Ess behind her. "Enough for today, I guess. Bye, Sam."

"Oh. Okay," said Sam, in a small voice. "Bye, Ess. Bye, Jinny."

Then, the day after that, Jinny got so sick of the shouting and moaning and the tiny fingernails scraping her skin, she marched out of the water almost immediately, with Ess clinging to her neck. But this time Jinny looked up and shouted at the sky, "I quit!" as she plunked Ess back on the sand. The girl stopped wriggling and shouting.

"Look," said Jinny, standing over her Care. "If you really don't want to swim, then I really don't want to teach you. Have it your way. We'll just keep you away from the water for now."

Ess grinned up at Jinny. She'd won, and she knew it.

"Yeah, well, don't look so happy just yet. If you don't want to swim, I'm finally going to pick the prickles out of your hair!" said Jinny, as she reached down to comb at the messy snarls with her fingers.

"Nooooo," shouted Ess, popping up and dashing off down the beach.

Jinny sighed. She knew this was an empty threat. She wasn't really going to deal with Ess's hair today either. It had gotten tangled, and there were sticky burrs in it from the prairie. It would take hours, and patience. Jinny didn't have either today.

9

Nice Work

The next afternoon, Ben handed Jinny a basket and said, "Hey, will you and Ess go to the tide pools for me? I need snails for dinner!"

"Really?" said Jinny. "Well, I mean, can't someone else?"

Ben looked surprised. "Why should someone else? You're not doing anything right now."

"Oh, come on. It's just that I've been fetching a lot lately, and I'm busy with Ess. She won't be any help in the tide pools, and she still can't swim."

"Oh, *perfect*," groaned Eevie from the other side of the kitchen. "Because you're too lazy to teach Ess to swim, you *also* get to be lazy about snail duty. That seems very fair. . . ."

Ben ignored Eevie, but he also shook his head at Jinny and

handed her a sack. “The tide pools aren’t deep,” he said. “I need your help.”

“Fine, fine, okay, sorry,” grumbled Jinny as she stomped off to collect Ess, who was digging happily in the sand with a stick.

“Hi,” said Ess brightly, looking up at her Elder. “I digging.”

“Yes, I see that,” said Jinny. “And you’re doing a great job, but Ben needs some snails for supper. I want you to come learn how to gather them.”

“Otay,” said Ess amiably, brushing sand from her knees and following Jinny down the beach and off to the tide pools.

Of course, Ben had been exactly right. Ess was delighted with the tide pools. Jinny showed the girl how to be careful not to cut her feet on the rough patches of coral and the barnacles, and she pointed out that the purple jellyblobs would sting if you let them brush against your legs when they floated by. Ess spent a while gazing at the beautiful petalfish, and then together the two of them gathered snails, setting them gently in the sack over Jinny’s shoulder. After a few minutes, Ess looked up thoughtfully and held out a delicate shell. “When we eat them, dey get sad?”

“What?” Jinny wasn’t sure what Ess meant.

“Dis!” said Ess. “Snail get sad, when I eat him up?”

“Oh,” said Jinny. “Well, no, he won’t be sad. Because he’ll be dead.” Was this something she needed to explain? She didn't think Sam had ever asked as many questions as Ess.

"Dead?" Ess looked into the shell closely.

"Yes, dead. He'll . . . stop moving. And be gone. He'll be chewed up and finished. Dead. Like a fish or an erster or a dried-out scuttle. Dead."

"Oh, no," said Ess. "Poor snail."

"Yes," said Jinny. "But the thing is, if they didn't die, we couldn't eat them. And then we'd be hungry."

"Oh," said Ess.

"Or if we *did* eat them, and they didn't die first, they'd wiggle in our guts and feel like *this*!" Jinny reached out and tickled Ess, grabbed for her little round belly.

Immediately Ess let out a barking cheerful laugh. She couldn't help it. "Hep!" she squealed. "No, Dinny! Stop it!" But she looked happy, so Jinny kept at it until Ess fell and splashed into the tide pools, laughing and wiggling.

"Anyway," said Jinny, looking down at Ess, sitting in the water up to her belly, "wait and see how good they'll taste with garlic and seaweed. Mmmm. Now, let's get back to work."

But the moment Jinny turned her back to pluck at a fresh batch of shells, Ess let out a shrill, earsplitting scream.

Jinny whirled around. "What? What is it?" All she could see was that the girl was thrashing and flopping, churning the water in the pool.

"No, no, no, no, no!" shrieked Ess as Jinny reached in to

grab her. But Ess was moving too quickly, like a fish herself, slippery.

"What?" shouted Jinny. "What is it? Ess? What *is it*?"

Then Jinny saw the eel, moving, slithering, trapped in the shallow water of the small tide pool, with Ess. Jinny's hands darted before her brain could catch up, thrust themselves into the water and grabbed for the thick dark muscle of a creature, lifted it from the water, and hurled it out to sea. Its twisting body looked like a bird in the sky for a moment before it smacked back down on the surface and was gone.

Jinny turned to Ess, scooped up the sobbing girl. "You're okay, Ess, you're okay, little fishy. I promise, you're fine. Nothing can hurt you. You're here, with me." She held the crying girl to her chest, amazed at how strong her own arms were, at how light Ess felt in this moment, even heavy with her drenched clothes. Ess continued to sob. "Shhhh," said Jinny. She stood, holding Ess, until the girl was only sniffling, trembling. Not knowing what else she could do.

At last, when Ess seemed calm, Jinny stepped out of the tide pool, wincing at the barnacles under her own feet. She walked back up onto the sand. "It's fine, she said. "You're back on the island. The island is safe. Ess is safe."

Ess looked up at her, rubbed at her eyes, and asked, "Safe?"

Jinny nodded. "Always and forever. The island is safe. You can fall and bump and scrape and even bleed a bit, but you'll be fine."

"But," said Ess, "that fish—"

"Eel," said Jinny. "That was an eel. And it wouldn't hurt you either. It might nibble a little, but that's all. I know it scared you, though."

"Out *dere*." Ess eyed the water—the tide pools and the waves beyond. "Dat's safe?"

"Well, no, not exactly," said Jinny. "That's a little different. The sea . . ." Jinny looked out at the water, at the miles of gray-blue that ended at the wall of mist. "The sea . . . can hurt you, if you don't learn to hold your breath and float and swim like the rest of us. Do you understand? The sea is different. It isn't . . . safe. It doesn't give second chances."

"The sea . . . ," said Ess, "will *dead* me? Like a snail?"

Jinny tried not to laugh. "Yes," she said. "I suppose the sea *can* kill you. But that's why you need to learn to swim. Because then it'll be fine. Then you can keep yourself safe. No matter what. Okay?"

"O-kay," Ess said. Though she still looked nervous.

"Now, that's enough talk about that for now. Let's get back to the others. I think we have enough snails, don't you?"

Ess nodded, and the two of them headed back, their snail-gathering lesson over. Jinny thought perhaps that was enough adventure for a few sleeps.

Walking back, Jinny tried to remember exactly how she'd learned about the sea. When she reached back in her memories, she couldn't find a single story. Probably Emma had told her this, had warned her of the sea, and taught her to swim, as all Elders taught their Cares to swim. But Jinny could conjure no memories of that lesson. Certainly there was no drowned child in her memory, no specific tale. She couldn't even picture what that would look like, a drowning. When she tried, she only managed to see a dead wet baby bird, like the ones that sometimes fell from their nests in the plomm trees. Still, Jinny knew it. They all knew it—that the sea was a danger, stronger than anything else. It fed them. It surrounded them. It kept them and defined their world. The island was only an island because the sea was there, all around. But the way the waves crashed against the cliffs and tossed spray into the air was *not* safe. Just the opposite. The sea was wild.

"How were the tide pools?" Ben asked, as they trooped into the kitchen, soggy and silent. "Did you have a good fetch?"

"Maybe better not to talk about it right now," replied Jinny, setting her sack of snails on the table. "I'll go back for more later, okay? Ess needs to dry off and rest a bit. It was . . . eventful."

Eevie, reading a book at the table, looked up at them as they passed. "What happened to you two? She looks like you drowned her. Nice work, Jinny!"

Jinny was in no mood. "I'll drown *you* if you don't shut up, Eevie," she hissed.

Ess gasped at that. "No, Jinny! No downing!"

Eevie smirked. "Like I said, nice work."

That night, after their dinner of snails and a quick story by the fire, Jinny took Ess back to their cabin and tucked her into bed. But she found she couldn't go to sleep right away herself. Restless, she rose from the bed, but when the springs beneath the old mattress creaked, she heard a small clear voice. "Dinny, pease stay?"

"Oh," said Jinny, "I thought you were asleep, Ess." She reached out to pat the girl's head, but when she did, Ess grabbed hold of her hand and wouldn't let go. "Pease stay. Or the sea might come. Don't let the sea get me, Jinny."

"Oh, Ess, the sea can't come here. You're safe on the island, I told you."

After a bit, Ess settled down, and her eyes closed, but Jinny stayed awake for hours, thinking. She had an anxious feeling of having done something wrong, though she wasn't sure exactly what it was.

"I'll do better, Ess," said Jinny. "I'll watch. I'll stick close. I'll be like that tree in the story. I promise. I'll give you everything."

10
Swim or Sink

The next day, Jinny and Joon were down at the dock, pulling up the nets, when Joon asked, "Where's Ess?"

"Oh, she's back in the cabin, resting," said Jinny. "I think it's better she not spend too much time near the water right now."

Joon laughed as she dropped a fish into the basket at her feet. "And how do you propose to keep her away from the water, Jinny? We live on an island."

"I know," said Jinny, untangling a long strand of dark kelp from the net in her hand. "But just for a few days, I think it's easier this way. She had a real scare yesterday, with an eel, in the tide pools. She's nervous about the water."

Joon turned and stared at Jinny. "Well, then, now is the

exact time for her to get in the water. Otherwise she'll never do it. You're just rewarding her fear. What are you thinking?"

"She hates it," said Jinny, shaking her head hard. "She really doesn't want to learn to swim. I know she needs to, after yesterday especially. She really needs to swim. But not today."

"Jinny," said Joon, in her firm, sure tone, "if you don't make her go back right away, she'll be even more terrified. Her memory will be worse than what actually happened. That's how fear works, right? It grows in your memory."

Jinny stared at Joon. "Look," she said. "You want to know the truth? I *can't* teach her to swim, okay? It's not just that she's scared, it's that I'm a terrible teacher, and I know it, and I feel bad about that, but it's the truth. I'm just not . . . patient enough. Or calm enough. Or . . . I don't know. I don't know how we all learned to swim. I don't remember it being so hard. Do you?"

Joon shook her head firmly. "No, but it doesn't matter how you feel, Jinny. This is about Ess. And you need to get over yourself. Because she needs to be able to swim. It's not safe—her crabbing and emptying the fishing nets, and living by the sea, not able to swim. Ben and I were talking about it. He says you told him it's one of the three main lessons, and yet . . ."

"Ben and you were talking?" Jinny was stunned. "About *me*? You think it's *my* fault? Haven't you seen me trying to teach her every day?"

"I know sometimes you like to carry her around in the

water, splashing and laughing. But that's not the same thing. And now it sounds like you've given up, quit on her."

"I didn't!" cried Jinny. "I'd never quit on her. I'm just taking a break while she gets over that eel in the tide pool. Anyway, you think *you'd* do a better job? You think it's so easy? Why don't you take a turn yourself then, *Joon?*"

"Are you saying I have your permission, then," asked Joon, squinting at Jinny and the sunlight behind her, "to try a different way?"

Jinny nodded. "If you think you can teach her to swim, go right ahead. Anytime. She's all yours. You'll see what I mean."

"Well, then, that's settled," said Joon. She glanced up at the path toward the cabins. "And look who's coming. Perfect timing," she said.

Jinny turned to follow the other girl's gaze, and saw that Ess was tumbling down the path along the ridge from the cabins, arms outstretched, kicking up dust.

"Well, okay, I guess," said Jinny, shaking her head. "But I'm not sure I want to be around for this." She reached down for the fish basket. "I'll go put these in the kitchen while you explain to Ess."

"Oh, I'll explain it to her, don't worry," said Joon.

Together the two girls walked down the length of the dock. Then Joon made for Ess, and Jinny trudged with her heavy basket of fish to the kitchen.

But a minute later, as she set the fish down on the table with a groan, Jinny heard familiar shrieking and squealing behind her. She whirled around. "Ess!" she shouted. "What is it? What's the—" In the distance her eyes found Joon, striding quickly back down the length of the dock, with Ess wriggling and kicking in her arms.

"Noooo!" Jinny shouted, and began to sprint. But it was too late. Jinny was nowhere close when Joon reached the end of the wooden planks and called out, "Good luck, Ess!" and tossed the girl neatly over into the chilly depths. *Plunk!*

"Aaaaggh!" Ess turned immediately into a flurry of water and flailing arms and screams, a shouting, choking disaster.

Jinny saw all this from afar, as she ran. She dashed forward, her heart racing, and hurled herself past Joon and straight into the sea, aiming for the churning arms and wet bobbing head of Ess, for the spot where the little girl was struggling to keep her head above the water.

But when Jinny popped up, head above the surface, a few feet away from her Care, she paused a moment, treading water, and stared. Because the girl was splashing less and paddling more each second. She was still calling and crying, choking water, alarmed. But now she also seemed to be . . . floating. Her hands churned and paddled in front of her. Her feet kicked out behind. Instinct had replaced fear.

Jinny glanced back over her shoulder at Joon. Joon stood on the dock above, arms crossed. "You said I could," she called out. "You gave me permission."

"Not for that!" shouted Jinny. "I didn't mean *that*. You could have killed her! She could have drowned!"

Joon laughed. "Hardly! Not with me standing here, ten feet away. It's not the open sea, Jinny. This little cove?"

"Well, you still scared her," shouted Jinny, wiping water from her eyes.

"Okay, sure," said Joon. "But it's better to scare her now then to lose her later. Don't you think?"

Jinny wasn't sure how to answer that. She turned back to look at Ess again. "Still!" she called out at Joon. "It wasn't your place! She's *my* Care."

"You weren't doing your job, Jinny," said Joon coldly. "Not sorry." Then she turned and walked away, up the dock, leaving Jinny and Ess alone.

Ess was now paddling in a straight line at Jinny. "Jinny, hey, Jinny! Look!"

"I see!" she called back, trying to smile, and clenching her hands together under the water to keep from reaching out to the smaller girl. To force herself to force the girl to keep swimming. "You're doing great. Are you okay?"

Ess looked pale and bedraggled, her wet hair like seaweed all around her face, But even so, she grinned and coughed out, "Yesss!" She paddled clumsily to Jinny and reached out for her, dipping under the water as she raised her arms to clutch Jinny's shoulders tightly. At last she hung there, limp and panting.

With Ess trailing from her neck, Jinny slowly swam back to land. She paddled toward the beach, puzzling all the while at what had just happened. Once they were in shallow water, Jinny stood and lifted Ess up, held her tightly. Then she began walking, and she didn't let go until they were back in the cabin. She walked slowly and carefully, her arms hugging the shivering kid, face resting on Ess's mop of wet hair.

That evening, while Ess was busy arranging shells in the wet sand along the beach, Jinny offered to help Ben with dinner. As she picked apart a pile of crabs for soup, Jinny looked up at him, stirring wild onions into a pot over the fire. "Ben," she called out.

"Yes?" he said, staring into his pot, as though looking for something in it.

"Joon said today . . . that you thought I wasn't doing my job. With Ess."

Ben turned, spoon in hand. His eyes looked concerned. "No, that's not what I meant," he said. "You're wonderful with her. She loves you. It's just the swimming. And other little work things, now and then. It's just that sometimes you don't seem to want to make her do the things we all *need* to do."

Inside, Jinny bristled faintly, but it wasn't the same as talking about this with Joon. If Ben thought it too . . . "She's *little*," said Jinny. "She's so little."

Ben came over to sit beside her on the bench. "She's exactly the age Sam was one boat ago, the age Nat was two boats ago," he said. "Everyone starts out little. And everyone gets big fast."

Jinny looked at Ben, into his eyes, which were watering from the onions. "Well, she can swim now, at any rate . . . ," she said.

"Really?" Ben smiled. "That's great, Jinny. Good work!"

"Thanks," she said with a sigh. "But here's an Elder lesson for you. It turns out that the best way to teach a kid to swim is to let Joon hurl her into deep water."

"Oh," said Ben. "Well, I guess, anyway . . . she can swim now. Good enough. Right?"

"I suppose," said Jinny. Then she added, "Ben, why do you think they sent Ess here in the first place?"

Ben wiped his eyes with the back of an arm. "That's a funny question to ask," he said. "I don't know. I guess I never really thought about us getting *sent* here. We just . . . come."

"Yeah—but someone must have sent Ess here, right? Dressed her? Put her in the boat? I mean, she wasn't born in it. So . . . why? Why did they send *any* of us here? Isn't it a funny thing to do, to put a little kid like that, who can't even swim, into a boat, and send her off on the water? Don't you ever wonder?"

Ben shrugged. "I don't know, but does it matter? I like it here. I love it."

"Well, sure, so do I," said Jinny, tossing down a crab shell.

"But I mean, did we do something bad, to get sent away?"

Ben snorted. "What bad thing could *Ess* have done?"

They both looked over at Ess, who was now doing something with a stick around her shells and humming a tuneless song to herself.

Jinny fidgeted with an empty claw, pulling the thin membrane inside it, to make it pinch Ben's arm. "Do you remember anything?" she asked Ben. "From before the island?"

Ben thought a minute, then shook his head. "Not really. Do you?"

Jinny shook her head slowly too. "Not exactly," she said. "But . . . sometimes I get a feeling, almost. Like I imagine a color or a shape. Or at night, in a dream—I see something in my head I've never seen on the island. But I can't remember exactly what it is when I wake up. The picture isn't clear. And it doesn't explain anything."

"I think probably," said Ben, "probably we didn't have anywhere else to go. I think probably we didn't have people to take care of us. I guess I think *that's* how we got here. We're orphans, right? 'Nine on an island, orphans all'? Like that wizard kid from the books? Or the boy with the gigantic peach? Only without aunts and uncles. Maybe this is where orphans go when they don't have aunts and uncles?"

"Yeah, orphans," said Jinny. "I guess I always thought that too." She paused before she added, "But the thing is—when Ess arrived, she swore she had a mother. *Mama*. She wouldn't stop talking about her. I guess that's why I've been thinking about this. Is that strange?"

Ben stood up and walked back over to the fire to stir his pot. It smelled wonderful, full of the onions but also ginger-root and wild garlic. He stopped to taste it before he said, "Mama, huh? I don't know. . . ."

"Crazy, right?" said Jinny, following him. "I mean, that can't be true, can it? A mama wouldn't send Ess away. Would she?"

Ben turned around, holding out the spoon. "I don't *think* so," he said as she sipped the broth. Then he added, "But it doesn't really matter, does it? Because here is where we all are. Here, with one another. In this nice place. With my delicious crab soup."

Jinny nodded, though she couldn't shake the feeling that it *would* matter. It *did* matter, to her. If Ess had a mama.

"Now dump that meat in, so we can eat!" Ben laughed.

Jinny rose to carry the crabmeat to the pot, but she couldn't bring herself to laugh at his joke. "Here *is* where we are. For now, anyway."

"Now that that's settled," said Ben, "can you go get me some sweet-weed, please?"

"Sure," said Jinny. "Of course."

As she picked the shiny green sprigs from the sandy patch that was their garden, Jinny thought about Deen, wherever he was. Did he know the answers to these questions now? She wondered what he was doing. She pictured him arriving in his boat, stepping out onto dry land. And then . . . what? What did he see before him? And who? Surely not a mama, surely not . . .

But what was it like there, in that other place? Who was there with him? Maybe he'd found Tate, and the two of them were off on an adventure together right now. For some reason, the thought of that made Jinny unhappy, though she knew it shouldn't. What would they do, in that other place, together, without Jinny? She couldn't begin to imagine it.

Jinny knew lots of things about the world out there from all the books she'd read. For instance, she knew about the constellations of the night sky, but the book hadn't said anything about the mist around the island that made the shapes the children saw at sunrise and sunset. Was that world different from Jinny's world? Jinny found herself tearing angrily at the sweet-weed, ripping it out in clumps, from the roots. She wasn't sure why.

11

The Truth Hurts

When Ess had been on the island for too many sleeps to keep count, Jinny woke one morning later than usual. The sun was up, and there were no dirty toenails scraping her legs. She propped herself on her elbows and looked around, but Ess was nowhere in the cabin. Only the collection she'd been assembling on the windowsill, of rocks, shells, dried flowers, and seedpods. Plus one broken bit of blue-and-white china with a bird on it, tumbled by the sea.

Jinny stared at the bit of broken china, her thoughts slow and thick with sleep, before she shook her head, climbed quickly out of the covers, and walked through the half-open door, still in her sleeping shift. She peered out and caught sight of Ess down by the water, holding a fat fish. Bent over her were Jak and Oz. Sam was watching too, from a safe distance, though the other three seemed not to have noticed him.

Oz was saying something to Ess, who appeared to be listening closely, though Jinny couldn't make out the conversation from her spot on the ridge. It looked like the boys were teaching Ess how to scale a fish, with a knife that glinted in the sun. Over and over Ess raked the knife sharply up and down the fish skin in a jerking motion. It made Jinny draw a quick breath each time. The older girl dashed back to the cabin to shuck off her shift and quickly pull on her day clothes.

When she sprinted down to the beach a minute later, she found the boys had moved on from scales to guts. "Now, when you've taken off all the scales, you make a slit there, near the tail," Oz was saying.

"Like dis?" Ess asked, jabbing the knife hard into the fish's taut belly with her tiny hand.

"Right there, yeah, that's it. And then pull the knife all the way up to the head, quick. But be careful!"

"Okay," said Ess. "I be careful." She made the incision, then dropped the knife sloppily in the sand beside her foot, just as Jinny arrived.

Jinny flinched when the knife hit the sand and stuck there, handle up. The sand could so easily have been the soft top of Ess's foot.

"Hey!" Jinny called out. "Careful with that!" But nobody seemed to be listening to her.

"Great," Oz added. "Now just reach up inside and give a good hard scrape with your fingers, so you get all the insides out at once. Yeah, like that. Nice job!"

"Yeah, nice job, Ess!" said Jak.

Jinny tried again to interrupt the lesson. "What're you guys up to?"

"Dis! I clean a fiss!" screamed Ess excitedly, holding up her gruesome handful of guts and goo. "See, Jinny! Dis! I do it my own self." The slime oozed through her fingers.

"Oh," said Jinny, trying not to retch. "Okay."

Oz grinned. "We were just showing Ess here how to clean a fish and some other fun stuff."

"Yeah," added Jak. "Other fun stuff! So she can help with dinner more."

"That's . . . nice of you," said Jinny. "Thanks. . . ."

"You're welcome," chimed both boys.

"Still," said Jinny, "can you check in with me next time? Before you teach her something like that?"

"Why?" asked Oz. He blinked.

"It's just . . ." Jinny thought briefly of Joon's swimming lesson, and of Ben's soft admonition. For a moment she tried to bite her tongue, but she couldn't manage it. The knife was so very mean and sharp, and Jinny was so bad at silence. "Just—I'm not sure she's quite ready to handle a knife that sharp."

"But I did!" insisted Ess. "I did it."

"Aww, c'mon, Jinny," laughed Oz. "She's fine. Nobody's ever gotten hurt *that badly* cleaning a fish. Have they?"

"Even so," said Jinny, "she's my Care, and I say she's too young. You can show her again later. Can't you? When she's older?"

"Ha. You're just jealous because you can't stomach it yourself. You've never been able to clean your own supper, and she's doing great."

"Yeah," added Jak with a teasing grin. "You just want us to wait until next year so you won't have to look at it. You just want us to wait until you're *gone*."

"Shhh!" hissed Jinny.

But she was too late. There was a tiny gasp as Ess dropped her wet handful of innards on her foot. Then she stared up at Jinny, one wet bloody hand outstretched. "Jinny go away?" she asked.

Jinny stepped over and bent down to scrape the girl's tiny toes clean with her fingers. "Pish!" she said gently. "Don't listen to anything these dumb boys say. They're only good for hunting and fishing and shouting and making a mess. They don't know what they're talking about. Now, come with me, okay?" She took the small slimy hand gingerly and led Ess away, glaring over her shoulder at the two boys.

Jinny marched Ess down the beach a ways, then led her to the surf, where she washed the offending foot neatly in the water. Jinny rinsed her own fingers clean, letting a handful of wet sand and tiny shell bits sift through them briefly. Then she turned and said, as if nothing had happened, "What should we do today, Ess? You want to go and visit the chickens? Have you had your breakfast? Maybe we can talk Ben into giving us some of those yummy snaps!"

But Ess wasn't about to be distracted by sweets. She stared at Jinny, her mouth drawn into a tight worried frown, her eyes huge.

"What?" Jinny asked. "What is it?" Though of course she knew the answer.

Ess kicked a foot at the shallow water.

"Look, it's fine," said Jinny. "*You're* fine. Now smile. Come on, silly!"

"But . . . ," said Ess at last.

"Yes?"

"But Jinny . . . *hafta* go away?"

Jinny sighed. She hadn't technically lied to the girl, but she'd certainly been avoiding this conversation. She wished she knew how Deen had told Sam about the rules of the boat. What words had he chosen for the telling? She wondered when the conversation had happened—how Deen had known Sam was ready.

"It's hard to explain," Jinny said with a shrug. "I don't want to make you sad. But, yes. It's true. I *will* have to leave. One day."

"*When* will Jinny go?" asked Ess.

"I'm not . . . sure," said Jinny. "Nobody knows. It happens when it happens."

"Jinny goes away . . . like Mama," said Ess. She did not ask this as a question. It was a statement. The tone of acceptance in her voice was flat, final.

"I suppose, a little bit," Jinny began. "I don't really know. But Ess . . ." And it wasn't what Jinny meant to say, but the words that slipped out of her next were "I'm not your mama. I'm just . . . *me*."

Ess's eyes filled with silent tears. "I know," she said even more softly, looking down at the thick cuff on her arm, her shoestring bracelet, which was now spangled with bits of shell and tiny feathers. "I know."

Jinny sighed. "This is hard. I don't think you can really understand what I'm trying to say. Can you?"

Ess looked up from the bracelet and stared at Jinny. "I unnerstand."

Jinny couldn't help being frustrated. There were so few words that fit the moment and so many feelings. She wanted Ess to understand that leaving, when it happened, wasn't her choice. That she loved the island and didn't want to go. Though at the same time, Jinny knew inside herself that she *did* wonder about the world out there . . . a little. She wondered where Deen had gone. It was all so confusing.

Meanwhile, Jinny's ankles, in their awkward crouch by the water, were beginning to ache. "You need to understand," she said, straightening up, "I'm *not* your mama, Ess. If I were, I'd never leave you. Never! Mamas don't leave their kids, unless they *have* to. Mamas are forever and ever. The problem is . . . here, on the island, mamas are only in books. Like dragons or birthdays. We take care of ourselves here, so we don't need mamas. Do you see?"

Ess scrunched up her mouth. "Mama's . . . not real?" she repeated softly, covering her bracelet with her hand.

"That's right," said Jinny. "You'll understand soon. I promise. That, and also you'll . . . forget her."

At that, Ess suddenly crumpled. She fell down in the wet sand, in the shallow surf beside Jinny. The choking sobs told Jinny just how wrong her words had been. But what could she do? Was she supposed to lie to Ess? Pretend there were mamas stored in a cave somewhere on the other side of the island? Or that a boat with a bunch of parents was going to magically arrive from out of the mist? Everyone kept telling her Ess could handle more, work harder, hear the truth . . . but now, when she tried that, *this* happened. Maybe Ess wasn't ready for everything so fast. Maybe everyone was wrong.

Ess continued to weep, and Jinny let her, unsure of what to do. When she couldn't stand it anymore, she sat down in the water and reached for the girl, set a hand gently on her back. Ess shrank from Jinny's touch at first, but something told Jinny not to take her hand away. Instead, she reached one arm around Ess's middle and pulled the wet child into her lap. With the other hand she pushed the thick tangle out of Ess's face. Then Jinny held her Care. Tight, firm. She crossed her arms over the girl's frail chest and rocked her in her lap, so that she could feel every tremble, every sob that shook Ess's body.

"I'm sorry," whispered Jinny into Ess's damp hair. "I wish it wasn't true. Or that I could remember what it feels like, so I could help you more. I can't be your mama, but I'm *here*. I'll be here when you need me. And I promise, you'll be okay. We all turn out okay. Don't we?"

Ess turned and looked at her, straight in the eyes. With words clearer than usual, she said, "Stay, Jinny. Peeze don't go?"

Jinny looked at her, remembering what *stay* had felt like in her own mouth, not so long ago. She grimaced. And she didn't mean to do it, but somehow . . . she nodded. It was a lie, the nod, and Jinny knew it, but it happened all the same. Jinny only meant to nod at the wanting. *I know you want that*, she meant to say with her nod. *I know how it feels to want that*. But she didn't think Ess had understood. She was pretty sure Ess thought she meant *I'll stay for you*, *like a mama would*, *forever and ever.* Which was funny, Jinny thought. Since nobody on the island had any idea how that would even work, or feel. Nobody they knew had ever stayed, or lasted forever.

In any case, Ess kept crying softly. Until. From some deep

place in Jinny, a song came creeping out, a small song, a quiet song, but a song she didn't know she knew. "Shush," sang Jinny.

"Shush, shush, shushabye hush.
Sweet little girl, be slee—eepy."

Jinny sang this song in a whisper and stroked Ess's forehead, and somehow her sobs became quieter, calmer, until at last she shuddered, then stopped, limp in Jinny's lap, leaning a small head against her shoulder.

Only then did Jinny stop to wonder if she'd made the song up or pulled it from some deep forgotten place. There was no way to guess. It felt conjured, like magic.

After a few minutes, Jinny looked around and saw that the others were watching from a distance. All of them, from different vantage points around the beach. Ben, stirring something in the kitchen, and Joon, mending a net with some prairie grass on a rock. Sam wasn't even pretending to do anything but listen and watch intently. Everyone's eyes were trained on Jinny and Ess, down at the waterline.

Jinny looked back at Ess and saw that her eyes were open again now, and the tears had stopped. "Hey," Jinny said gently, giving the girl another squeeze, "I think you've got everyone a little worried." She pointed down the beach, to where Nat and Eevie were watching them with armloads of driftwood and solemn eyes. "How about a smile? Let them know you're okay? What do you say to that?"

Ess limply lifted her head from Jinny's shoulder. "Okay, Jinny," she said softly, with a sniff. "I smile." She forced a quiet smile, an attempt.

Jinny touched the smaller girl on the nose and said, "That's only a tiny little bit of a smile. I want to see a great real smile, a sloppy smile! Do you have one in there for me?" Ess looked unsure about that, but then Jinny gave her a tickle in the ribs, and uncontrollably Ess burst into squeals.

All down the beach, the other kids heard the sound and breathed again. Work resumed. Ben clanked and stirred in the kitchen. Joon whistled as she braided.

As if on cue, Oz and Jak ran toward them. Oz called out, "Hey, Ess, Ess! Want to play with us?"

"Oh, jeez," said Jinny. "What do you think those rascals want now?" She rolled her eyes and Ess laughed. They both stood up, dripping, and turned to greet the boys.

"We thought maybe Ess would want to play Grab a Crab?" Oz called out as he ran up, holding out two particularly big, angry-looking crabs, brown claws snapping.

"Yeah," echoed Jak. "Grab a crab!"

Ess squealed and pointed at the creature. "It's pinchy!"

"Yep!" Jak grinned. "Pinch, pinch, pinch!" He made his own hands into claws and pretended to pinch Ess in the belly until she laughed out loud, a grunting, easy laugh.

It wasn't a game Jinny would have chosen, but she could see how awful Jak and Oz felt. They were trying to help, and she knew it. They only wanted to make things better. "Well, I suppose we could give it a try," she said.

Ess clapped her hands and spun in an uncontrollable circle. "Yes. Me, me, I grab!" she shouted as she spun.

"Hey, I'm sorry," Jak whispered, hanging back to talk to Jinny as Ess followed Oz up the beach. "For what I said."

"Thanks, Jak," said Jinny. "But it's not your fault. It's not anyone's fault. I just don't want to make Ess cry. But I guess it's like Deen used to say—I don't always get what I want."

"That's not *exactly* what he used to say," Eevie said, snickering as she walked up. "Not *quite*, anyway."

"What?" Jinny turned to look at the girl's sharp, smug face. Why did Eevie have to wrinkle her dumb nose like that? "What do you mean?"

Eevie squinted at her. "Deen used to tell the rest of us, 'You don't have to give Jinny what she wants. You just have to let her think she's getting it.'"

"He said that?" demanded Jinny.

Eevie nodded.

"Really?" Jinny whirled around and asked Oz and Jak. "Did he say that to you guys too?"

Oz and Jak looked at each other and shrugged.

It was an awful moment, but all around her, the others were gathering for the game, so Jinny tried to push what Eevie had said from her mind. She could only handle so much before breakfast.

Then Oz shouted out, “Okay, make a circle, everyone—here we go!”

And Jak repeated the shout, “Here we go!”

Soon everyone was suddenly shouting, “Here we gooooo.” Moments later, Oz released his angry captives and sent a huge crab scuttling straight at Jinny.

Startled, she reached out and grabbed for the crab. She darted forward and gripped the beast by its shell, then raised it into the air, claws waving furiously. When she released the animal again and sent it off in Sam’s direction, she gave a shout so loud she surprised everyone, including herself.

“Aaaaagh!” she raged into the air.

Everyone stopped for a moment, to look at her.

“Did it pinch you?” asked Sam. “Are you okay?”

Jinny just shook her head. “Nope,” she said, looking the other way. “Not a bit.”

12

Keeping Count

Jinny wasn't certain what made her start counting her sleeps. She only knew that some deep urge made her take up her knife one morning and carve a small notch into the doorpost of her sleeping cabin. It made a thick soft sound, *shoonk*. Jinny stared at the notch, and at the knife in her hand. She wondered why she'd done it. *Funny*.

From books, Jinny knew that the world out there counted time—in minutes and hours, days, weeks, and months. Decades and centuries. But on the island, there were only sleeps. Snaps dried to candy in ten or twelve sleeps. Every twenty sleeps or so it was time to change the bedding. But no one really counted beyond that. They figured a year was the number of sleeps it took the green boat to return to the cove.

But nobody was certain whether their years were equal to each other or not, because nobody had ever thought to keep track, that Jinny knew of.

Jinny knew that counting her sleeps wouldn't change anything, really. The notches in the doorway couldn't keep the green boat from appearing, full of some drippy little boy she'd never even know but hated already.

Still, it was oddly satisfying to see the notches grow in the weathered wood. She liked to run her fingertips along the grooves as she came and went through the door. The counting felt good to her. It was something, anyway, a thing she could do, a kind of knowledge. The notches were reliable. Steady. Permanent. Counting them was a comfort.

One day there were ten notches in the wood.

Then there were twenty.

By the fiftieth notch, Ess had learned to swim well and to relight the fire with a flint. She had learned to wash her feet at night without being told, so Jinny no longer had to shake the sand from her blankets in the morning. Ess had also learned to speak in nearly full sentences. She had learned to make seaweed stew all by herself. And for the most part, Jinny had learned to believe that Ess *could* do these things. She didn't worry so much.

Jinny tried to remember to invite Ben along anytime she was going to show Ess something new, but that sort of thing tended to be unplanned, to happen when it needed to happen.

“I’m sorry,” Jinny explained to Ben when he asked how she’d taught Ess to repair the fishing nets. “Oz showed her, actually—it wasn’t even me this time!” And that seemed okay. Ben seemed okay.

When Jinny reached her hundredth notch, she ran out of room and had to move around to the other side of the doorframe. Now, when she made the groove each morning, she felt a tremble in her belly. One hundred seemed like a very large number, and at the same time, the hundred notches seemed to have appeared so suddenly.

The morning of her two hundredth notch, Jinny woke to the sound of rain, spittering softly against the sand and leaves outside her window. On the island, rain was usually something that happened for brief minutes in the night, while everyone slept. It was rare to have a rainy morning. Jinny looked out the window and wondered at it. She nudged Ess with her foot. “Ess, hey, Ess, wake up!”

The little girl rolled over and buried her face in her pillow. “Oomph,” she said. She began to breathe heavily again into the cloth.

Jinny kicked harder. “Get up, Ess. Look, it’s rain, *day* rain!”

“Rain?” The girl sat up groggily and rubbed her face with the back of a hand. She looked out the window. “Rain.”

“Isn’t it nice?” asked Jinny. “I’ve got an idea! Let’s grab a nibble and then curl up in the book cabin, to read the morning away and listen to the rain. Okay?"

Ess nodded, and the two girls pulled on their day clothes and opened the door. Outside, everything smelled wet and bright, alive. Together they ran through the rain. Ess laughed the entire way, sticking out her tongue as she ran. "Ahhhhhh!"

In the outdoor kitchen, the fire had gone out, so Jinny and Ess just grabbed a big handful of swinks and another of nuts, slamming the metal boxes shut quickly.

"Ach, we're out of snaps again," said Jinny. "But I guess this'll do us for now, right?"

Ess nodded., "Yes. This'll do us!" Her face was already smeared with swink juice, her mouth full and happy. She followed Jinny up the wet sandy path to the book cabin. But when they pushed open the door, the girls found Nat and Eevie already inside.

"Hey," called Nat, looking up from a small bowl of dried snaps on the table beside her.

"You're the culprit!" shouted Jinny, laughing and reaching for a treat. "Look, Ess. Snaps!"

Eevie only grunted. She was squinting to read in the dim light from the overcast window.

"Move over," said Jinny, wiggling her wet way onto the couch beside the two girls. "Make space."

"Hey, no way!" said Eevie, looking up. "There's not room for everyone, Jinny. And we were here first. Plus, you're getting too big, especially *some* parts of you." She pointed at the top of Jinny's tunic, which had begun to swell out in a way that nobody else's did.

"Shut up, Eevie," snapped Jinny, crossing her arms over her chest. "Anyway, Ess and I will be more comfortable on the floor. Right, Ess?"

Ess didn't answer. She'd already pulled a book from a stack and plopped down on the woven mat. She began to turn the pages.

Nat smiled from across the room. "What have you got there?" Ess held up a worn and ragged book, with a picture on the front of a sleeping monster and a sailboat. "Oh, that's one of my favorites. I've always thought that place looked a little like our island. Why don't you read to us?" She settled back to listen.

Ess looked up. "Jinny can read it," she said.

"Of course she can," Nat said with a smile, "but I've heard Jinny read plenty. I want to hear *you* read it!"

Ess shook her head. "I can't. I don't."

"What's that?" asked Nat. "What do you mean you can't?"

Eevie looked shocked. She spun to look at Jinny and said, "She's not *reading* yet? What have you guys been doing all this time?"

"I . . . everything else," said Jinny. "There's a lot to learn. You have no idea how much. Anyway, it's none of *your* business."

Jinny turned back to Nat. "Honestly, I know she should be

better by now, but it's so hard, and we *are* working on it. The reading is just . . . going slowly."

"Slowly?" scoffed Eevie. "You're running out of time, you know."

"Let's not talk about *that* just now," said Jinny. She raised her eyebrows and jerked her head in Ess's direction, sending a warning. "Okay?"

Eevie rolled her eyes. Nat said nothing and went back to her book.

Jinny glanced at Ess, who was gently turning the colorful pages in her lap. As she opened a book herself, she tried to push away the thought of Ess's reading, but it kept circling back, distracting her from the words on the page. It wasn't that Jinny hadn't *tried* to teach the younger girl to read. It was just that she wasn't a very good teacher, and Ess wasn't a very willing student. It was like the swimming all over again, but Jinny wasn't quite sure what to do about it. There was no way to just throw Ess into a book the way Joon had chucked her into the sea. Instead they sat each day and stared at books together, and Jinny ran her finger underneath the words as she read them aloud, hoping Ess would learn. She sang her the alphabet at tooth-brushing time, and also in bed at night, but the girl just didn't seem to be getting it. Between the two of them, they'd only succeeded in giving up.

Now Ess looked up from her book and pointed at something on the page. "Jinny! What does Abigail say? Here!" She shoved a grubby finger at the page. Jinny leaned closer, to peer over the little girl's shoulder, and read what Abigail had scribbled in the book.

"Ummm, yeah, right here, after the part about how Max climbed into the sailboat and sailed away, she's written, 'What kind of dumbbell runs away from home, just because they have to go to bed without supper?'" Jinny stopped for a moment, stared at that line, considered it. Then, flustered, she flipped a few pages, stopping when she saw more pencil marks. "And here, after the part about how Max sails back home again, she's written, 'If only it were so easy.'"

Ess was quiet for a long moment. Then she asked, "What's *supper?*"

"I've always assumed it was kind of soup," offered Nat.

"Oh," said Ess, nodding. "Okay." She added, "I like Abigail."

"Yeah, me too," said Jinny. "But I wonder how she knew so much about everything. I wish I could meet her and ask."

"Well, *I* don't want to meet her," said Eevie, setting down her book and reaching for another.

"Really?" asked Nat. "Why not? She's smart. And funny."

Eevie frowned. "But that's just it. She thinks she's *so* smart. She thinks she knows *everything*. And she's written something in every single book. Like everything in here belongs to her. I hate when I'm reading and I stumble on Abigail. Why would she do that, write in all of them?"

Nat shrugged. "I don't know. I guess I always thought they were her books to begin with."

"Really?" said Jinny. "You mean you think she brought the books here, to the island? Like, when she came in the boat? I never thought about that."

Nat nodded. "Yes, that's what I always thought. Anyway, I love her scribbles. It's like I know her."

"I feel like that too," said Jinny. "Like she's one of us, even though she's gone. Like she's managed to stay on the island forever, in a way."

"Except that she didn't stay, did she?" added Eevie. "She left like everyone else does. And like that King Max. Now she's probably old or dead, and nobody even remembers her. Even her books are falling apart. They've been here forever, and they're dying. I wonder if Abigail is dying like her books."

"Ugh, what a morbid thing to say," said Nat.

Jinny stared at Eevie and wondered what made her the way she was. She was smart, but not in a nice way. Jinny couldn't remember if Eevie had always been a crank, if she'd arrived on the island like that.

Jinny glanced at the window, then stood up and reached out a hand to Ess. "Hey, Ess. It looks like the rain is letting up. Let's go. I just remembered something fun I saw Deen do with Sam when he was teaching him to read, something that might help us." Jinny pulled Ess to standing beside her, then dragged her through the door and back out into the day. She waved without looking back. "Bye, Nat. Have a nice morning. Bye, *Eevie*," she called over her shoulder.

Outside, the rain was gone, but the sky was still cloudy. Jinny walked Ess past the sleeping cabins, down the path to the water's edge, where the sand was hard and wet. There, with a long stick she drew a letter in the wet sand.

"Okay, so . . . here we go. *A* is for *abalone*," said Jinny. "Ah—ah-abalone. *A*."

Ess giggled at her and jumped into the wet sand, making footprints.

"Come on, Ess. Stop messing around. Don't you want to know how to read? Like the rest of us? Like a big girl?"

Ess shrugged.

"This is an *A*," said Jinny. "Can you at least say *A*?"

"*A*," said Ess. "*A* for *ahhhhhhhbalone*, *A* for *Ess*."

Jinny sighed. "Not exactly, but almost. Let's try again. *A is* for *Abigail*. Here, you try to draw an *A*."

"*A* for *Abigail*!" shouted Ess, reaching for the stick.

"Good," said Jinny. "Now make an *A*. Make ten of them. And each time you make it, say aaah aaah *Abigail*!"

Jinny watched Ess make her letters, her tongue clenched between her teeth, as though she was concentrating very hard. After a bit Jinny sat down, then lay back on the sand and felt the damp hard grit beneath her, through her wet clothes. She closed her eyes and thought about the books in the book cabin.

Like all the other kids, she'd read everything she could get her hands on. The books were fun. The books were a welcome distraction. But the books were actually far more than that. The books were from the other place, the world out *there*. The books were about *that* world, and when the boat came for Jinny, she'd find out what was real in the books and what was make-believe.

Jinny had read about ballerinas, girls who could spin on their toes. She'd read about pyramids, triangles of stone, with dead people buried inside them. That pyramid book had made everything sound true, but it was hard to imagine pyramids being real. Why would anyone go to the trouble of building with stone, only to place a dead body inside it? That seemed crazy.

Jinny had also read about wars, unicorns, and something called chocolate, but she couldn't even begin to picture any of those things. Was there really a world out there of stone triangles full of dead bodies and girls spinning on their toes? In books, there were giant metal boxes with wings that soared through the sky, carrying people. Surely that couldn't be true. Just thinking about it brought the tightness back to Jinny's belly. And a funny tingle to her scalp. She shivered it away.

Jinny propped herself up on her elbows for a second and saw that Ess had lost count of her letters. She was still making *A* for *Abigail*. There must be thirty of them in the sand, crooked letter after crooked letter. But that was good. Ess would know *A*, at any rate. That was more than she'd known when she woke up this morning. Maybe in twenty-six notches, if they kept this up, Ess would know her letters.

Jinny felt a little ashamed of how long it had taken to bother with writing out the alphabet. She'd just sort of expected the kid to figure it all out on her own, as they read together each day, but now she saw it was going to take more work than that.

Jinny thought about Abigail. It had never occurred to her that Eevie, or anyone else, might truly dislike the notes in the margins of the books. She'd heard Eevie grumble about it before, but Eevie grumbled about so many things. Jinny had never taken that seriously, especially not when she, Jinny, loved the notes so much. Jinny remembered reading a book about a family traveling across a prairie of grass in a wagon, and how she'd come across a scribble that day from Abigail that read, "Thank goodness they took the wolves off *this* island before we got here!"

She was so grateful to Abigail for this snippet. That there had been wolves on the island, wolves! And that *they* had cleared them out. Whoever *they* happened to be. She wondered how Abigail knew about it. Abigail seemed to know so much.

It felt like a secret, this fact that once there had been wolves on the island. And also that there was a time *before*. Jinny couldn't imagine that. How long ago was *before*? she wondered. How many years had the books been there? Eevie was right. The books were dying. They were falling to bits, year by year. How long had it been since they were new, since Abigail?

How long would they last? Had anyone else—maybe Deen—ever thought these crazy thoughts? If he had, he hadn't shared them with her. Jinny swung her head and looked out at the ocean, where it vanished into the mist. It had never occurred to her that Deen hadn't shared everything with her.

Jinny stared out at Ess in the sand, now abandoning her *A* in favor of a shape that looked more like a flower with a long tail, sort of like the fire flowers in the morning sky. Ess was drawing a picture. So much for the alphabet. But that was all right. Tomorrow they would work on *B*.

13

Treading Water

Five notches later, Ess had mastered the letter *A* and the letter *B* but gotten no further. "*A* for *apple*!" sang Ess, drawing with her stick in the wet sand. She had never actually seen an apple, but for some reason they appeared in lots of books. People were forever eating apples or putting them in pies. "*A* for apple and *A* for *ahhhhhhhhhhhhhhh*!" she screamed. "And *B* for *bee* and *B* for *bzzzzzz*!"

"Yes, that's great," said Jinny. She was going out of her mind from boredom. "Let's try *C* again before dinner—what do you say?"

"*C!*" shouted Ess, "*C* for *sea*!" She drew a wave in the sand. Ess always drew a wave in the sand. Jinny groaned.

"Hey, Jinny," called Joon, striding down the beach toward her from the dunes, Eevie at her heels. "Can we talk to you for a minute?"

"Of course," said Jinny, grateful for the distraction. She walked over to the join them. "What is it?"

"We were thinking," said Joon, in a quiet voice. "Well, Eevie was saying . . . that you might like some help, with Ess. With . . . her reading."

"Oh, thanks for offering," said Jinny. "But it's okay. Ess is my job. I'm responsible for her, not you. And we're working on the reading right now. See?" She pointed down the beach at Ess but then noticed the little girl had abandoned her letters, and was now seated and burying her feet in the sand.

"Yes . . . I do see," said Joon. She didn't look impressed.

Jinny stared at Ess. Then she turned back to look at Joon, and at Eevie, who had perhaps been instructed not to open her mouth. Jinny couldn't remember her ever keeping quiet for this long before. She was bouncing lightly on her toes.

Jinny squinted at the two girls standing in front of her. "You *really* want to help me with Ess, with the reading?"

Joon nodded. "If you'd like," she said. "Look, we don't want to upset you. We don't mean to criticize. We're really just offering to help. You've been working at it so hard the last few days, and you seem . . . frustrated."

"You think it's like the swimming, I guess?" Jinny said, glancing down at her feet. She felt a little embarrassed, but it was generous, what Joon was offering to do, and she *was* frustrated. Very.

Joon shook her head. "No, really. No judgment. We just want to help."

Eevie said nothing, and Jinny was fairly certain *she* didn't just want to help. More likely she wanted to show Jinny up. But it amounted to the same thing if Jinny didn't have to spend the rest of her life going over *C* is for *cup*.

Jinny threw up her hands. "Fine!" she said. "Sure. I guess. Why not?"

"Really?" Joon smiled.

Jinny nodded. "Honestly, I *detest* this. And I'm discovering I'm not . . ." She looked at Eevie, hating the moment. "I'm not good at it, teaching. I can admit that. And you got her swimming, after all. So, sure, do whatever you want, and thank you. Just . . . can you go somewhere else? Away from me, while you do it? I could use a break."

"Sure!" said Joon. "Of course. That's fine. I was worried you'd be annoyed. But I promise I'm just trying to help. I know she's your Care. We all know that."

Jinny shrugged. "I don't want to fight with Ess anymore."

"*I* don't mind fighting with Ess," Eevie said with a grin.

Jinny rolled her eyes. "It's not like we *fight*," she said. "*Fight* isn't the word. Ess doesn't fight. She just doesn't listen to me. She wanders off. It's like trying to teach a kitten to read, or a scuttle. And I hate making her do things she doesn't want to do."

Eevie snickered. "You never minded before Ess. Bossing *us* around." Then before Jinny could think of what to say to that, the other girl had bounded off down the beach, toward Ess. "Come on, Joon!" she called back over her shoulder.

Ess wasn't exactly excited to join the two other girls for yet another lesson, but in the end she straggled off behind them, leaving Jinny oddly alone on the beach, with nothing to do, for the first time in as long as she could remember.

At first Jinny just sat there, listening to the water and the birds wheeling above. It was so still, so empty, without Ess. Lonely, but peaceful. Off in the distance, she could hear Oz and Jak shouting about something, but there was nobody who needed her, nobody she had to take care of or think about. It was a funny feeling.

Then . . . Jinny felt restless. She looked around. She tried to think of something to occupy herself. She could go for a walk, of course, but she'd walked every foot of the island a million times. She could go to the sea-star field, but it didn't seem fair to do that without Ess. She could do chores but didn't want to.

Really, there was *nothing* to do that she hadn't done countless times before. There was no cliff she hadn't scaled, no food she hadn't tasted. Nothing she couldn't do with her eyes closed. The more she thought about that fact, the more restless she felt. Itchy.

It had been different with Deen, at least until he'd started acting so quiet at the end. Deen had always had an idea for something new to do. Odd, wonderful things. Once he'd buried her up to her neck in sand, just to see if he could do it. It didn't sound like a fun thing to do, thinking back now. But it had been, with Deen. Deen made everything fun for years and years. Deen and she sat and talked or picked berries or carved sticks, and that was plenty. Jinny didn't want to carve a stick by herself.

The more Jinny thought about it, the itchier she felt. As though she was falling deeper and deeper into a hole. At last, she stood up and stretched. She walked down the beach a ways, but her itchiness walked with her. The feeling swelled inside. Hot and obvious, automatic. Jinny wanted to shout. She kicked at the sand as she walked. Hard.

After a little while, Jinny reached the spot where all the shoes were buried, where the white bone tree stuck up into the sky. Jinny looked at the pile of shoes, the tree, the island rising behind the beach. Then she turned around, away from the island, to stare at the sea, and she watched the waves roll in, watched the sun glint on the endless vista.

Jinny felt her anger subside. Quickly, she reached down and untied the drawstring on her pants. There *was* something she'd never done. She'd never swum alone. Not ever. And she'd never swum *out*. Past the shallow waves that lapped the shore. Never in all these years. Not even with Deen.

"See?" Jinny muttered. "I didn't always get what I wanted."

Beneath the waves, she knew, the sea was a universe all its

own. Full of hidden creatures, rocks, and even mountains. It was another world. Just thinking about the miles and miles of watery unknown sent a shiver down Jinny's spine. There was fear in her shiver. But not only fear.

Jinny stepped out of her loose pants and kicked them aside. She raised her tunic over her head, let it fall on the sand beside her. She tiptoed into the warm shallows and then kept going, striding out into the gray-blue. When the water was high enough that the small waves broke against her bare thighs, Jinny ducked down and submerged herself, until the chill was gone from her bones, and her skin felt smooth and good, the same temperature as the water.

Then Jinny began to swim, slowly, carefully, evenly. I'll just go until I get tired, she thought, then I'll turn around and come back. I just want to see what it's like to swim far. I couldn't do this with the others. But I can do this alone. Jinny touched a foot down, to see how deep the water was, and she found she could still touch, but beneath her feet, the sand had turned to a muddy, squishy surface, riddled with strands of weed and bits of shell.

She began to swim again, and after a few minutes, the water temperature dropped, causing her breath to catch. Then she got used to the cold and swam faster, harder. Jinny stretched out her arms. She cupped her hands and struck at the waves. She swam and swam, and her arms grew tired, but only a little. She closed her eyes against the salt sting and kept on.

At last, Jinny felt her breath weakening, so she turned to float, belly up, to rest on the ripples. What a wonderful feeling it was, to be alone like this, on top of the ocean and beneath the sky. She felt like she could float forever. Jinny wondered if maybe, somewhere, on the other side of the sea, Deen was swimming right now, both of them in the same water. Only an ocean between them.

Suddenly, a small wave rolled over her and filled her mouth and nose. It sent her coughing, so she turned back upright and treaded water for a second, wiping the splash from her eyes with one quick hand. And when she did, she saw . . . something. With her salty, blurry eyes, she saw a shape, a smudge of green. Her breath stopped and she peered to see the smudge better.

"No!" cried Jinny. "No!"

The boat? It couldn't be—not now, like this. What was happening? Jinny began to swim back, away from the green smudge. She swam hard.

Then another wave rolled over her, and when she looked up and peered around again, the green smudge was . . . gone. *What?* Jinny rubbed at her eyes, but she still couldn't see the boat. Where had it gone? Had it not been the boat after all? What *had* it been? Some sort of greenish dolphin? *Had* it been at all? Was she seeing things?

That must have been it. Just her imagination, a trick of the light on the water. There was nothing to see, nothing. Only the sea, a flat line in the distance, and the mist above it. In every direction, nothing. Nothing all around.

Then it hit her what *nothing* meant. Jinny whirled around again and realized what she couldn't see, what else wasn't there. Somehow, the entire island had disappeared, vanished into the mist that wreathed it.

"W-wait!" Jinny sputtered as she turned quickly this way and that, small waves rolling past her, breaking gently against her shoulders. "How can it just be gone?" she cried.

It was. Gone from sight. All the land. Her whole world. Everything she knew. Some combination of the mist and the distance had left Jinny stranded in the sea. Directionless. *Now* she felt the cold. *Now* her teeth began to chatter, and her legs began to cramp. Her entire body felt covered in prickles, and her arms were suddenly tired. Heavier than they'd ever been before. The feeling of moments before, that proud strength, that brave aloneness, was gone, replaced by cold fear. This was *alone* too. She was paralyzed, treading water with feet of stone. But even if she could tread and float forever, night would come. Jinny couldn't imagine floating in the darkness, in the cold, with only the stars for company. And eventually, she'd need to sleep.

She longed to swim again, to strike out and stop treading, but she didn't know which way to head. There was nothing to tell Jinny where the island lay, nothing to mark it. And if she swam in the wrong direction, where would she end up? If she tried for home and got it wrong, she'd only end up farther away, heading for open sea.

Jinny thought of Ess, of the girl's sad face, if Jinny disappeared. If Jinny never came back. What had she been thinking, swimming alone this way? She was afraid for herself, of course. But also, *she* was the Elder. She owed Ess more than this.

Meanwhile, Jinny was getting tired. So she turned and floated some more, hoping for a thought, an instinct, or best of all, a glimpse of the island through the mist. Jinny stared up at the forever blue of the sky and waited. She waited for something to happen.

Then something did happen. Not off in the distance, but right there, beneath her, Jinny felt a tremble. She felt a wave that came not from afar but from below, a shift in the water, a pressure at her back. Something moved, big and dark and invisible. Something pushed against the water and the rhythms of the tide.

Jinny startled and flipped herself up, tilted upright with a gasp, as her arms beat the surface, became a sudden frenzy, and her head jerked back and forth in all directions, searching, hunting, wondering. What?

Jinny saw nothing. But then she *felt*. What was it? A brush, a touch. Jinny felt a slick tight skin glide past her, rub against one of her bare thighs. She screamed. It brushed her again. Whatever *it* was. It moved fast. It felt solid. It was a flank, a wall, a small bit of something vast. Jinny turned her head sharply in every direction, found nothing but the sea. Only now she knew she was not alone. There was something near. With her, beneath her, maybe all around her. Panic filled Jinny's chest, her lungs, her head. Fear and spit filled her mouth, and her arms flailed. But where to go? There was nowhere to go. Only endless water.

Then Jinny saw something. A difference. A ripple that became a shape. Jinny watched as the something broke the surface. Cleaved the sea in two. It was as though the blade of a knife was rising from the water, sharp end up. The knife sliced the water, and grew, and kept rising, until it was a great wall, a jagged cliff, a triangle of what looked like stone above her head. It was a fin, it had to be, a massive fin, bigger than anything Jinny could have imagined. Jinny treaded, paralyzed, as she watched it rise, and tower. Her breath froze inside her. Her flesh froze too.

As quickly as it had risen then, the fin dipped back down, sank beneath the gentle waves. But the water all around Jinny felt charged now. The currents shifting, as though something was swirling and swimming, creating eddies under the surface.

Now, Jinny swam. In a split second she struck the water. Eyes closed, heart racing. She didn't think, but swam like a body, like a creature, like a fish. An animal moving fast, churning her arms, kicking her legs, moving to move. She didn't pick a direction. The direction picked her. The direction was *away*. That would be enough, to be away. From this.

In a matter of moments, Jinny let out a cry. A sharp sound rose from her throat, or maybe from someplace else inside her. She saw the island appear through the mist, as though it had been waiting for her all along. As if she only had to wish for it. As if the island was inevitable. As if it would have been there for her, no matter what direction she'd swum. Home. She only had to want it badly enough. Nothing had ever been so welcome as that glimpse of land, that pale sand beach, the cliffs above. Jinny had never been so eager for anything in all her life. She swam and swam for land. She pushed her tired body, propelled it somehow through the water.

Jinny could feel herself crying as she swam, taste her tears, salty as the cold sea but warm on her face and tongue. She wept as she swam home. Home. Home. Because if she wasn't moving, she was done.

And just as she thought that her breath was breaking, that the blood might burst through her ears, Jinny felt her feet touch bottom, and she let herself collapse. Let her body drop into the water, felt the tide carry her gently back to the safe, sturdy ground. There she rolled a moment in the shallow surf and lay panting, with the welcome grit of the beach on her cheek. Could anything be so wonderful as the firm wet sand of the island? Why had she ever thought to swim away?

Jinny lay still, waiting to catch her breath. When she could finally stand, she dressed her sodden shaking body in the dry clothes, warm from the sun, and began to walk, trembling with the cold and the exertion and the fear. Now that it was over, she couldn't stop shaking.

When she walked into camp, she found the others were all eating at the table. Laughing on their benches, chewing and sipping, as though life was no different than it had been an hour before. As though everything was fine.

Jinny stared at them. She'd been in another world and returned. She'd been *away,* and *away* was the opposite of this. *Away* was danger, and Jinny knew now how danger felt. Staring at the table of familiar faces, Jinny felt like she was watching everyone else through a sheet of water or a thin fog. She didn't feel ready to speak. As happy as she was to see them, she didn't feel ready for any of this. Her sore body wanted to collapse again, into her own soft bed, sleep. She couldn't talk, could only stare at them, mute.

But Ess shrieked and pulled Jinny back. "I did it!" screamed Ess. "Jinny! I readed words!"

"Huh?" Jinny couldn't remember how to speak.

"I readed!" shouted Ess again.

"Oh," said Jinny. "Yes. That's nice, Ess." Jinny still couldn't fully process anything Ess was saying. Then Jinny remembered the reading lesson, and she found she didn't care very much. "That's great," she added distantly. "Good job."

Ess chortled. "I readed *all* of the words. *Cat* and *bat* and *mat* and *fat*."

Jinny forced a smile. "Great, Ess."

Joon nodded. She looked right at Jinny, just like she always did, like nothing was different. "She did well. I think you'd already taught her more than you realized."

"That's great, really great . . . ," said Jinny, her voice drifting off. She turned to head for her cabin. She was very tired. "Okay. I'm going to bed. Good night, everyone."

Behind her, Oz was chewing and muttering to Jak at the same time. "What is it with Elders? They always get so weird at the end, don't they?"

Eevie agreed. "Yep, she's acting just like Deen did, isn't she? But also Jinny's jealous. *That's* why she's skipping dinner, I bet. She's sore because *we* helped Ess, and *she* couldn't."

Jinny stopped walking. She glanced over her shoulder, and when she saw triumph in Eevie's eyes, it was as though something snapped inside Jinny. She heard Eevie's grating, jangling voice, and it pulled her back into the world. Her fog cleared, and Jinny felt herself turn to Eevie.

In a calm smooth voice that didn't feel like her own, Jinny spoke. "What's *wrong* with you, Eevie?" she asked. "Why do you have to ruin everything? Always? You make it impossible to love you."

The others stared. The two girls argued often enough, but this was different. This voice was new for Jinny. Thin and sharp as the razor edge of a mussel shell. Her words too jagged, too true.

"Jinny?" Ben said, standing and raising a hand to stop her.

But Jinny couldn't stop. "It's like you're hungry," she said in that same cold, strange voice. "Like you're hungry inside all the time, and you want to eat us. Like you want to chew us all up. But why? What made you hungry like that? What happened to you?"

"Jinny," gasped Nat, standing to place a soft hand on Eevie's shoulder protectively. "Jinny, stop."

Suddenly there were bright tears in Eevie's eyes, and she only looked small, young, and bruised. "It isn't . . . always so easy, you know," she choked. "It isn't always so easy to be happy. I *see* the rest of you happy, and I don't know how you do it, but I try. It's hard for me. But I *do* try. To be happy, and nice."

Everyone was silent, frozen, staring from one girl to the other.

Jinny knew she'd gone too far. Somewhere inside her there was a squeak of sympathy, a softening. But after the long swim, the terrible knife fin rising above her, the away and apart and alone, she didn't have the energy, the heat for this moment. She was certain her body would fall over if she stood for even another minute, that if she tried to care now, her skin would break and shatter.

"All right, then," Jinny said, with a faint nod. "All right,

Eevie. I'm going to bed. Ess, you come whenever you like."

Just like that, she walked away.

Jinny was halfway up the path, striding fast, before she realized that Ben was behind her, huffing to keep up. She turned.

"Jinny!" he called out, stopping on the path and bending over to catch his breath. "I thought . . . you might need to talk?" He peered up at her, red-faced and hopeful.

Jinny looked down the hill at him. It was so nice of him, she thought, to worry. Ben was so nice, always. And yet his niceness made her feel almost as tired as Eevie's meanness. Annoyed, even.

"No," she said, trying to keep her own voice kind. "No, I really just want to sleep now, Ben. Good night."

"Are you sure? I mean, we could . . ."

Jinny didn't have it in her to talk to him. She turned away. Ben *couldn't* understand how she was feeling. How could he, when she didn't even understand it herself? She'd never felt this way before. She didn't know what to call it, so she walked away and didn't look back. How long he stood there, watching, she didn't know. She didn't care enough to notice.

14

A Good Day to Disappear

Because she'd gone to sleep so early, Jinny woke early too. It was still dark out. She lay in bed, staring at Ess beside her, and trying to remember the day before. So much had happened. *Too* much had happened. Jinny felt raw and exposed, yet her memories were vague. She remembered mist all around, the island gone. She remembered the green smudge and the creature, whatever it was, with its terrible fin, rising above her. She remembered her fight with Eevie. Why had she said those things? What had come over her?

Jinny felt nervous, edgy. She wasn't ready to face the others. She wasn't sure if she was angry or sorry. So before the sky was even light, Jinny sneaked down to the kitchen, packed a basket of snacks, and returned to the cabin for Ess. Just as the usual ribbons of gold were beginning to braid the sky, Jinny led her groggy Care up the path and into the prairie. The two of them. Alone. It felt like a good day for a long walk. It felt like a good day to disappear.

And it was. Together the two girls roamed. They picked swinks and ate until they couldn't eat any more. Jinny showed Ess how to make chains from the purple bursts of wild clover that grew in the grass. They climbed the cliffs and lay in the sun. They paddled in the shallow stream that ran through the prairie, where tiny silver fish nibbled their toes. "Deen used to swear they were trimming his toenails for him," she told Ess. "I *almost* believed him. But I think he nibbled them himself."

"Eww!" shouted Ess. And they both laughed. But Jinny couldn't help feeling like part of her simply wasn't *there*, with Ess, in the prairie. Like her shadow was gone, or some other layer of herself. As much as she wanted to be present, she felt like she'd left part of herself behind somewhere—maybe in the sea. Though it wasn't the sea she thought about, or the dark fin rising above her, but rather the vision she'd had of the small green boat. When she closed her eyes, it was the green smudge she saw, heading toward her. It made her heart race to think of it.

Many hours later they returned, and Jinny felt better. She was worn out from walking and running and swimming, and her tiredness felt good. She found she wasn't mad at Eevie anymore. Still, she headed straight for her cabin. She didn't want to lose this easy feeling. She wanted to hold on to it for a while. But as Jinny opened the cabin door and stepped inside, Ess peered longingly down at the beach, where the others all seemed to be playing a game of catch with a ball of rags.

"Want to play?" she asked Jinny, her brow wrinkled.

Jinny smiled, but she shook her head. "Sorry, Ess. I will later. Maybe tomorrow. But right now I just need some rest."

"Oh," said Ess.

"*You* can go, if you want." Jinny nodded toward the game. "It's fine. Really. I just think I want to stay here. Read for a bit."

Ess stared back at the cove, where the others were running and shouting, laughing out loud. Then she turned back to Jinny and shook her head. "No. I want to stay with you," she said.

"Really?" Jinny was surprised. "Thank you," she said, and meant it, deeply. Even if part of her wanted to be alone.

So Jinny stepped into their cabin, shook the dirt from her feet, and sat on the edge of her bed. As Ess crawled up and curled beside her, Jinny gave the girl a quick hug. She was glad not to be alone just now after all. Very glad.

After that, Jinny reached for a book, and for a long while she read aloud about a little girl with a pet horse and a monkey. It was a wonderful story, one of Jinny's favorites, and Ess listened intently. But at some point, Jinny's voice drifted off, and her eyes fluttered shut. She fell into a dreamless hole, a thick inky sleep. She'd been up since before dawn, and her body needed rest. It took what it needed, as bodies do.

Until something woke her.

A sound. Even in her groggy state, Jinny knew what it was. The sound echoed inside her. It spoke to her. And something inside her rustled and woke. It was as though she'd been waiting for it—the bell. As though she'd known it was coming.

"No!"

She sat up in bed.

No.

Beside her, on the floor of the cabin, Ess was playing with her family of sand dollars. Lining them up like a long thin train, in some very specific order Jinny couldn't fathom.

Ess looked up at Jinny, startled to hear her shout. "Did you have a bad dream?"

Jinny didn't answer. What could she say? She jumped down and hopped over the line of shells, then scrambled for the door. It couldn't be. It couldn't be. Not *yet*. She wasn't ready. And after yesterday . . . No!

But it *was* time, and Jinny knew it. She *had* known, for sleeps and sleeps, she realized now.

When Jinny stepped from the cabin into the late-afternoon sun, she squinted.

Ess trailed behind her, still clutching a sand dollar. "Jinny, wait!" she called. "Wait for me!"

Jinny looked back at her Care. She paused, stretched out a hand.

Along the beach, everyone else was running for the cove. Just like every other time the boat had come. Every other time. Only this *wasn't* like every other time. Not even close. This was *her* time. It was Jinny's turn. Everything felt different, even the air around her—magnetic, charged. She had never been so unready for anything. Had Deen felt like this? She couldn't imagine. She remembered that day, so well, so sharply. The gray sky. How sad she'd felt, how hard it had been. The catch in Deen's voice, the look in his eyes. And yet he'd gone. Even when she'd asked him to stay, he'd gone. Because that was what people did when their turn came. They left.

Now it was *her* turn.

When Ess slipped her fingers into Jinny's, Jinny gripped them tightly. Together, they walked down the beach, to join the others in the cove. But slowly, slowly. Not running at all.

Everyone was lined up. They stood waiting for Jinny. Nothing could happen without Jinny. Oz and Jak stood, clutching their knives. Nat and Eevie, side by side, both looking nervous. Ben, with an arm around Sam, and Joon, standing slightly apart, holding the horrible bell. When Jinny and Ess finally arrived, Joon set the bell on its hook and shot Jinny a look she didn't completely understand. *Good-bye*, it said gruffly. And maybe *I'm sorry*.

Off in the distance, through eyes squinted against the

bright sun on the water, Jinny could see it, the small green boat appearing through the mist, just as she'd pictured it. Like a memory. The water was calm in the flat, happy sunshine. Nothing like the vast, angry sea she'd been lost in only the day before. It was amazing how different the sea could feel from one moment to the next. It was amazing how different Jinny herself could feel.

She tried to remember all the other times she'd stood this way, but besides Deen's leaving, she found they all blurred. "Emma," she said out loud. But it didn't help. She couldn't conjure up a clear memory of that moment, or her Elder, really. Tate . . . that was clearer.

She looked down at Ess, at the bits of leaf and sand in her hair and the smudge on her cheek. She looked around her, and everything felt wrong. All wrong. This was too nice a day for leaving. It was a day for napping, for sitting still, for clover chains, and picking swinks in the windless sunshine. They were going to have root soup for dinner, Jinny's favorite. She could smell it in the air.

Root soup. Why was she bothering to think about soup?

Jinny felt Ess trying to wriggle her fingers and realized that her own grip on the girl's hand had become too tight. She relaxed but didn't let go.

"Jinny, what is it?" asked Ess. "What's happening?"

But Jinny couldn't stand to look down, make eye contact. She still hadn't managed to explain any of this to Ess. Why hadn't she prepared the girl? What had she been waiting for? It would only be worse this way. Jinny knew that now. She got it, too late. Someone else—probably Ben—would have to talk to Ess about this. Poor Ben. It suddenly hit her that she really hadn't done her job as Elder, hadn't told Ben all the things he needed to know. He'd asked and asked, and finally given up. And now it was his time, and there were things she hadn't told him. What had she been thinking? What was wrong with her? How had she let Ben down this way? Jinny felt her belly begin to cramp. She wished she could bend over, fold herself in half, but she stood up straight. She forced herself.

They all waited in silence and watched the boat come in. It made a beeline for the very spot where they were standing. Soon Jinny could see the child who would replace her. A white shirt and a blur of brown hair. For a brief moment, she hated him, this boy. As the boat drew nearer, she could see his hair was curly. He was crying, of course, and snotting. He came quickly, and in moments, the boat was digging its trench in the wet sand at their feet.

The boy blinked, and Jinny gasped, startled, as she saw that his eyes were blue. Like her own, apparently. Jinny had never seen blue eyes before. Was this what she looked like? Was this what other people saw when they looked at her? It was strange, mesmerizing. The boy's eyes nearly glowed.

Beside her, Ben coughed, and Jinny glanced over at him. He looked at her sadly, and stepped forward, because that was his part this time. He knew that much. This was his job to do. As it had been hers last time. Ben reached out his arms and lifted the boy from the boat. He set him down gently in the sand beside Ess.

Everything was happening too quickly.

"Welcome," Ben said. "Welcome to our island." Then he stepped back and it was Jinny's turn.

She knew what she had to do. What she was supposed to do. If only she could make her feet listen to her head. This all felt so familiar. So much like the day that Deen had left. One year ago. Everything on the island was ruled by this moment, measured by proximity, either before or after, to this moment. Jinny hated it, hated the boat. Still, she knew she had to step forward. It was time. It was *her* time.

Jinny stepped. She turned, as Deen had turned, to face the others. This was her chance, to face them all. The line of them. Sad faces, even Eevie's, even after last night. Nothing else mattered now but that they were her people. Her family. So familiar. And she had to leave them. Jinny felt the cramp inside her turn to a sharp pain beneath her ribs, as if she was a fish being gutted with a small, sharp knife. As if everything inside her might spill out onto the sand at her feet.

Jinny took another deep breath. "I guess . . . it's time," she said. Her voice caught in her throat, trembled. The roof of her mouth felt strained, unnatural. It was hard to speak, but she forced out more words. "I guess I have to go now."

Ess made a choking noise. "Jinny, you hafta go?"

Jinny closed her eyes briefly, then opened them again and nodded. "I do."

There was a sob, a torn sob as Ess brought her hands up to cover her face. "No! Why?"

Jinny began to shudder. She couldn't handle it. This was too much. She looked away from Ess, up at Ben. Ben would be okay. Ben was safe. Ben would get her into the boat. Somehow.

"I'm sorry," whispered Jinny, still staring at Ben, though she was speaking to Ess. "It's too late now to explain, Ess, but Ben will help you. Okay?"

Ben nodded gently.

Ess whimpered.

"I'll miss you so much," said Jinny in a shaky voice. "*All* of you. I'll miss the stories and the fire and the fishing and the prairie and the games we play. I'll miss everything." Her eyes filled and her heart broke. "Everything, everything, everything."

Ess spoke. "Stay," she said faintly.

It was like an echo. And in a flash, Jinny was back a year, back on the beach, and the boat was there. The day was gray and overcast, and it was Deen leaving, and Jinny calling out, "Stay!" Only—Deen was leaving anyway. He wasn't listening to her. He *wasn't* doing what she asked. He was angry, until suddenly he was gone.

"Stay?" Jinny repeated after Ess in a whisper. She found

the girl's eyes, and held them with her own. Then Jinny looked down at the line of them, all of them. She forced herself to make eye contact with each of them, as best she could. One by one by one.

Ben, kind Ben. Holding her warmly in his gaze, even though she'd let him down. He nodded at her, and it was too much to bear. Jinny's eyes darted to Sam. The little boy stood staring at his feet. He was sniffing wetly, and Jinny was certain he was thinking of Deen. Sam still remembered this moment. Too clearly.

Next Jinny glanced at Joon, her eyes on the horizon. Pretending not to care. Impatient for this to be done. Because it was hard. Jinny understood that feeling.

The two boys together of course, the brave loud hunters, shoulders squared, chins up. Jak wouldn't cry unless Oz did. Jinny flashed them a quick smile. She moved on to Nat. The girl's eyes were closed, hands clasped behind her back. Jinny knew Nat would miss her but also that she'd accept this, as she accepted everything.

And then there was Eevie. Jinny looked at Eevie and was surprised to see there were tears on her cheeks. "I'm sorry," she mouthed at Jinny. She buried her face in her hands.

Last of all Jinny shifted her gaze back to Ess. She took in the small face framed by an unruly dark halo. Ess's chin was shaking as she cried. Her arms were crossed over her chest, but through her tears, she stared at Jinny, unblinking. Waiting, like the rest of them. Though she didn't understand—how could she? Jinny hadn't prepared her. Jinny hadn't done her job for Ess any more than she had for Ben. She'd let them down, and now she'd abandon them. Sail away. Because she didn't know how to do anything else. Because *nobody* had ever done anything else.

Jinny stepped forward and leaned down to hug Ess. She felt the thin bones shaking in her arms. She let go quickly, turned. She couldn't bear this anymore. She couldn't. . . .

Jinny wished she could undo the moment. She owed Ess more than this. She owed Ess a real good-bye, an explanation. At least that much. If only there was time. If she had time, she could do this better. But there was no time left. And now Ess would forget her. *Ess would forget*. Jinny would be forgotten.

She turned to face the boat.

She took a step.

She took another step.

She leaned forward and stared out at the water beyond the boat. The cold water shrouded in mist. Full of dark fins like knives, vast creatures beneath. Jinny shivered.

And then . . . before she knew what she was doing, she had pushed the boat sharply away. Out into the water. Empty.

"Jinny?" asked Ben in his measured voice.

Jinny ignored him, kept her back turned to him. Watched the green boat drift for a moment.

"Jinny?" Ben repeated himself. "Are you okay?"

Still Jinny ignored him. She was watching the boat, waiting for it to wander, to float out to sea. "Shhh," she said, a finger to her lips.

The problem was that the boat didn't drift. It sat for a moment a few feet away, as though confused. Then it zipped right back up to the shore beside Jinny's legs and gave a gentle nudge, bumped her shin softly. "Ouch," she whispered.

"Jinny?" asked Ben one more time.

Now Jinny grabbed the sides of the boat forcefully and stomped out into the water until it was up to her knees. She pulled the boat along with her as she waded farther, until the water was up to her waist, until her tunic pockets filled with air. She pushed the boat again, as hard as she could, away from her.

The green boat tried to double back again. Jinny grabbed it and gave it a shake. "Go!" she shouted at the boat. "Go home!"

"Jinny," called Ben again from the shore. "This is crazy! What are you doing?"

"I'm staying!" said Jinny, slapping the side of the boat wetly, sending a splash up into the air. "Can't you see? I'm not going. Except the stupid boat isn't listening to me."

As if on cue, the boat zipped back past Jinny again, up to the sand.

Jinny stomped after it. "Stupid boat. Do as I say. Go home!"

"Can you do that?" asked Eevie. "Can she do that?" But nobody answered.

"Jinny?" Ben reached out to touch Jinny's shoulder as she came back ashore.

She shrugged off his gentle touch. "Leave it alone, Ben."

"Jinny," Ben urged. "This . . . isn't what's supposed to happen."

Jinny flipped around and shouted. "I don't care! I'm not going. You don't know where the boat goes. You don't know what's out there. It could be horrible. Out there."

Ben urged. "You just have to believe in it. You just have to trust."

"Trust who? Why? Why should I trust anyone? There are no reasons, only rules. Why should I get in a boat just because it happens to show up one day?"

"Everyone else has done it," said Ben.

"So what? I'm not everyone else. Maybe everybody else has drowned."

"Maybe they haven't."

"Anyway," said Jinny, "the Elder lessons. You aren't ready. I've done . . . a bad job. I still have to tell you things."

"I'll figure it out," said Ben sadly. "I'll do my best."

"Well, Ess. She needs me. I don't want to let her down. And she isn't ready," said Jinny.

"She's ready," said Ben.

"She's sad. She's crying! Look at her."

"We all get sad. We all cry," said Ben. "But that doesn't mean we won't be okay. You have to go."

Jinny set her hands on her hips. "Make me," she said firmly.

Ben stared at her for a long minute. Then he said slowly and softly, "You know I won't do that, Jinny."

Jinny stared back at him. Ben was so gentle. He took such care of them all. But right now it was too much care. "Yeah," she said at last. "I know."

"Don't do this, Jinny," said Ben. "What do you think will happen now, if you do this thing? If you stay? Please . . ."

Jinny stared back. "What do *you* think will happen, Ben? What? The *sky will fall*, like in that silly rhyme?"

Ben shrugged. He looked worried. "I don't know. Maybe."

"Well," said Jinny, "I guess we're about to find out." And she turned back around. But this time when she reached for the boat, instead of sending it back out to sea, she pulled it up onto the sand.

Almost as if it could read her intentions, the boat fought her. It pulled and struggled. It wanted to be in the water. It belonged in the water. But Jinny was strong, and the boat was a boat. In the end, Jinny managed to drag it all the way up onto the beach. "There," she said with finality, drying her hands on the shoulders of her tunic.

Standing on the sand, looking around at all the shocked faces, Jinny felt a tremor. Though she couldn't be sure if the tremor was inside her body or in the world around her. Maybe it was both. Maybe *everything* was shaking.

Jinny pivoted to inspect the new boy, the lump in the sand, sitting exactly where Ess had sat a year before. "Enough of this!" she shouted lightly, tossing her hands in the air. "Enough about the boat. New topic. You! Who are you? What's your name?" She stomped up and stood right in front of him, her hands on her hips.

The boy gazed up at Jinny. Though his face was wet, he didn't look scared. "Loo," said the boy, pointing to his own chest.

"Well, welcome, Loo!" Jinny called out in a loud false brave tone. "Welcome to our island. You'll love it. I'm Jinny. Now, how about we all go get a snack?"

Loo nodded, and Jinny reached for his hand with one of hers. With the other she grabbed hold of Ess, who looked utterly bewildered. "Let's go," said Jinny. And she marched back toward the fire circle with the two smallest children firmly in her grasp. They had to run to keep up with her.

15

Ben's Turn

If things had gone as usual that night, the other kids would have withdrawn to their cabins, leaving Ben and Loo to get acquainted. Instead, Ben silently served up nine bowls of root soup, and then, finding himself out of bowls, poured his own dinner into a pewter mug and drank it down. They all ate more quickly and silently than usual that night, with their eyes on the new arrival, who seemed strangely at ease, and made a huge mess of his soup, not so much eating it as spilling it.

On the other side of Jinny, Ess sat extra close, so that their elbows brushed each time Jinny scooped another spoonful of soup. She glanced down, and Ess gave her a soft smile and bumped her elbow into Jinny's again. There was that, at least. But when Ess spilled her soup, getting up from the table, and

Jinny moved to help her wipe up the puddle, Ess said quickly, "No. I can do it my own self." Jinny didn't understand, exactly, but she felt like everyone was watching her, so she just nodded and went back to her dinner.

Usually, on the night after a Changing, the kids wouldn't have gathered at the fire circle after dinner, but Jinny hadn't left in the boat, so everyone was a little unsure of what to do. What was supposed to happen now? Jinny took the lead and started for the fire. And though the job of storyteller would have otherwise gone to Ben, it was Jinny who picked up where she'd left off the night before, reading from a book about an intergalactic traveler in love with a rose.

Though they all did the same thing they did every night, there was tension in the air, a nervous silence. Nobody argued or joked. Oz and Jak didn't shove or punch each other, and even Eevie offered none of her usual commentary. Sam looked stricken. Only Loo was squirmy, fidgeting and grunting. He seemed to be struggling to sit still, itchy in his skin, so after only a few pages, Jinny closed the book and said, "Let's make it an early night, shall we?" There was an audible sigh of relief as everyone rose from the fire circle to seek the privacy and rest of their own cabins.

When she stood up, Jinny reached automatically to her right for Ess's hand. Then she reached to her left for Loo's. "Come on, guys!" she said to them both. "You look tuckered. Let's get you to bed."

Eevie looked over sharply at that. "Wait, what?" she said. "Are you taking Loo?"

"Um, yeah," said Jinny, across the dying embers. "I'm the Elder."

"But it's Ben's turn," argued Eevie. "Isn't it? Isn't Ben the Elder now?" For some reason she looked to Joon for help.

Joon nodded, a thin frown on her lips. "That's right," she said.

"No!" said Jinny, shaking her head in confusion. "That's not right."

"Of course Eevie's right," said Joon. "You got Ess, Jinny. Loo belongs to Ben. You know that. It's his turn."

Loo looked up each time someone said his name, glancing from speaker to speaker. His mouth hung slightly open as his bright eyes darted keenly.

"But," said Jinny, "I'm oldest. So I'm Elder. I'm in charge. That's what *Elder* means. Ben only becomes the Elder if I leave. There can't be two Elders." She looked over at Ben. "Right?"

Ben didn't answer her. It was awful. Jinny had never seen him look at her like he was looking at her right then. She was suddenly out of breath. "Look," said Jinny, glancing around the circle, "I'm not trying to take anything away from Ben. It just makes more sense. This way, Ess and Loo can play together. Plus, I have experience at this now, and Ben doesn't know all the things I do. He doesn't know all the Elder lessons yet—"

"Whose fault is that?" asked Eevie.

Jinny didn't look at Eevie, and her eyes fell to the ground. "Anyway, Ben has a lot to do already, with the kitchen."

Even as the words left her mouth, Jinny wasn't sure why she was fighting for the boy. If she stopped to think about it, two Cares just sounded like a lot of work. But standing there by the dying fire, facing Eevie and Joon and the others, Jinny felt as though she'd walked too far down a path to turn back now. Like she'd be admitting she was wrong about *everything* if she changed her mind about this.

"Where will he sleep?" asked Ben softly in a practical tone. "You don't have room for three in your cabin."

"Sure I do," said Jinny. "It'll be fun for them to share." Then she had a thought. "I know—I'll just borrow the cushions from the sofa in the book cabin. Ess and Loo can have my bed, and I'll sleep on the floor, on the cushions. All right?"

Ben just shook his head, looking at the sand.

Eevie frowned. "Not really."

Joon stared at Jinny, but said nothing. Jinny could feel her judgment.

Everyone else was silent too.

"Well, anyway," Jinny said again, breaking the silence, "I'll just go do that, get the cushions, before it gets any later. We could all use a good night's sleep."

She didn't wait for anyone to answer her this time. She didn't want to argue, and she didn't want to look at Ben's sad face. Did *none* of them want her there? Did they all just want her to leave forever? Nobody even seemed happy she was staying. Except Ess.

As she sprinted up the path to the book cabin in the darkness, Jinny told herself it would all be fine. "This isn't bad," she said to herself as she opened the door. "It's just different. It'll only take getting used to. They're all just confused right now. It'll all be fine."

However, when she attempted to dismantle the old brown sofa she'd spent so many hours lounging on, Jinny found that even the cushions didn't want to cooperate with her. They were stitched to the frame, and no matter how she pulled, they didn't want to come off. In the end, she had to fumble around in the darkness outside the cabin for a sharp-edged shell to cut the cushions loose. It took a while sawing at the cloth with the clumsy shell, and she ended up ripping the cushions quite a lot. Jinny, staring at the ragged brown fabric, knew she'd never be able to put things back the way they had been, but at last she had the three large cushions gripped awkwardly in her arms. That was something.

Then, just as she was turning to leave, Jinny happened to notice a slip of white paper sticking up from the side of the couch frame, pale in the dim room. It had been covered by a cushion and was now exposed, but what was it? Jinny dropped the cushions, leaned over to tug the paper free, and was shocked to discover herself in possession of a sealed packet.

When she heard a noise at the door, she instinctively slid the envelope into her pocket. "Hello?" she called out.

"Jinny," said Ben in the darkness, his voice sharp but quiet.

"Oh, hi," said Jinny awkwardly. "Do you maybe want to help me with these?" She picked up a cushion and held it out to him, though when she looked up, she found she couldn't meet his eyes. "Never mind," she said.

"This isn't how it works, Jinny," said Ben, surveying the ragged cushions and the destroyed couch. "Or . . . it's not how it's *supposed* to work. Can't you see that?"

Jinny shook her head and said, "What makes you sure you know so much, Ben?"

"I *know* you're scared to leave," said Ben gently. "I can tell. And I know Ess doesn't want to see you go. But you still have to follow the rules, Jinny. We all do. Can't you see that? I don't know why you're doing this, breaking all the rules . . . but it's not fair, to anyone. It feels . . . wrong, and dangerous."

Jinny didn't answer. She only moved forward, walking past Ben and out into the night, dragging the cushions behind her into the path. She blinked, and was surprised her cheeks were wet. "*What* rules? We don't have any idea why we do what we do. None at all! Nobody ever told us anything."

Ben followed after her. He stood in the doorway, stared out into the starlight. "Maybe that's true. There's a lot we don't know. But this, what you're doing now, it doesn't fix anything. It only makes a mess. Everyone is scared down there tonight.

In a way they've never been scared before. You know that, don't you? Can't you see it? You're letting everyone down."

"I'm doing the opposite!" cried Jinny, stopping and turning back to face Ben again. "And anyway, we're all lost here, stranded. Like a shipwreck or something. At least I did something when I had a chance. I made a choice."

"Yes," said Ben grimly. "You did, didn't you? You made a choice, for *all* of us. Whether we liked it or not. You got your way, Jinny. What else is new?"

That made Jinny halt for a moment. She blinked. "But . . . ," she said, "I didn't want *my way*. And I wasn't trying to hurt anyone. I just didn't want to leave, and abandon Ess. . . ."

Ben continued. "You weren't thinking about anyone but yourself, Jinny. You say you're staying for Ess, but are you really? You're staying because you want to, because you're scared. You can't just do whatever you feel like whenever you want. It's not fair."

Jinny looked up, startled. Ben's words were an echo in her head. She remembered Deen saying the very same thing. It felt like so long ago now.

"I don't do whatever I like!" she shouted, the words louder than she intended them. She lowered her voice. "I'm not selfish. And *you* don't always know everything."

"You may not be a selfish person," said Ben, "but you're being selfish now. I don't think you thought much of me, or Loo, did you? I've been looking forward to taking care of him, Jinny. I've been waiting years for this. There are different ways to let someone down."

"You don't even know what it's like," she argued. "It's not that much fun, having a Care. Teaching them everything—swimming and reading. It's hard. And some part of them is always dirty or dripping. They break things. They smell."

Ben sighed. "I like taking care of people. And anyway, *fun* isn't the point. Would you give up having cared for Ess? To have more fun?"

Jinny didn't answer. Of course she wouldn't give up her time with Ess. And Ben was right—he would be a wonderful Elder. She knew that. And she knew it was her fault he wasn't ready. "You can take the next one," she offered.

Ben groaned. "But this was supposed to be my year. Next year I'll be gone. Or am I supposed to stay because you stayed? Are you just going to keep the boat forever, up on the sand, until it falls apart? And then we all get old and die on this island?"

"I . . . don't know," said Jinny. She hadn't thought it out like that. She hadn't really thought it out at all. "Is there a better place to die?"

"So then, is Joon supposed to stay too?" asked Ben. "And Oz after her? *All* of us? Together forever? Until Loo and Ess are alone here? And our world is over?"

Jinny cringed at that thought. She didn't have an answer for Ben, so she stared up at the stars she knew so well, and her voice was a whisper when she said, "This is my home, Ben, and nobody can make me leave it. Nobody can make me go. I'm not going out there, *away,* and I'm not leaving Ess. I'm sorry if it makes things hard on you. You can leave if you want to. Right now. You can take the boat."

"You know what?" said Ben thoughtfully. "I think you feel bad now. I think you're just embarrassed to admit you were wrong."

Jinny stared at him as she adjusted her grip on the cushions and began walking. "I'm sorry you're upset," she called over her shoulder. "I really am. I didn't mean to hurt you. But I'm done talking about this."

"I'm sorry too," said Ben, his voice fading into the night.

Back in her cabin, Jinny found that someone else had settled the two small kids into her bed together, tucked them neatly in. They were both snoring lightly when she arrived, and Jinny couldn't imagine who had done it. It was the sort of thing Ben might have done to help, under other circumstances, but Ben had been with her. Oh well, she thought. It didn't really matter who had helped. She was grateful, in any case.

Jinny settled her cushions on the floor, a makeshift bed. She was ready to collapse. But when she went to change into her sleeping shift, something rustled in her tunic pocket, and she remembered the packet. She pulled it loose and held it up to examine it in the weak moonlight from the window.

There were no words on the front or back of the envelope,

nothing to identify it. Jinny ran a finger along the sealed flap. For a moment she sat, looking at the creased paper, listening to the two children breathing in the bed. It felt wrong to open something that had been closed for so many years. But she knew she was going to do it. She took a deep breath, tore the edge carefully with a fingernail, and slid out a folded sheet of paper.

The sheet felt crisp and smooth, and there were tiny flowers in each corner. Jinny had never seen paper like that before. She ran a finger over it softly and found the flowers were raised. The gently looping script was pale gray on the creamy paper, too faded to make out in the dim room.

Jinny stood up and held the sheet of paper in the moonlight that shone through the window, but even then, she couldn't read the words. They were too faint. For a moment, she thought to take it out by the firelight, but then she might run into someone, and they'd be sure to ask what she was holding. No, this was her secret, for now. She'd wait for sunrise.

Jinny put the letter back in the envelope and slipped it under her makeshift bed before she settled down with a faint groan. The cushions felt lumpier on the ground than they'd been on the couch, and they kept sliding apart beneath her. But she was so drained it didn't matter. As she drifted off into the oblivion of sleep, she thought to herself that she'd have to find a way to lash the cushions together with rags or dune grasses in the morning if she was going to keep sleeping on them. She'd find a way to make it better. Somehow.

16
Lemons?

Jinny woke up with one arm limp and wobbly, full of prickles. Her back was sore too, from where her cushions had slid apart in the night and she'd fallen through to the rough plank floor of the cabin. It had not been a good sleep.

She shifted herself, tried to shake the feeling back into her arm. When she could put her weight on it again, she rearranged her cushions and rose so that she could crane her neck to peer into the high bed. Jinny smiled at what she saw. Both kids were curled in a messy heap together, snoring soundly, black hair mingling with brown, arms in a tangle, mouths open. They looked happy in their dreams. Maybe everything would be fine. Maybe this would turn out well after all.

But however glad Jinny was to see them sleeping, she

couldn't help feeling a little jealous of them, up there in the soft bed. With a useless sigh, she rubbed her face and settled back again on her lumpy cushions, letting her exhaustion wash over her and her eyes flutter shut. As tired as she was, Jinny couldn't force herself back to sleep, couldn't turn off her busy brain. She wondered what would happen now. Eevie would probably be spiteful. And Joon would glare in silence as she had the night before, chin tilted up, nose in the air. Jinny sighed just thinking about it.

At the very least, with the benefit of sleep and sunlight, Jinny knew what she needed to do next. She owed Ben an apology. She *didn't* always need to get her way, and she'd prove it. She'd fix her mess and make things right. Just because she'd stayed didn't mean Ben shouldn't have his Care. He could take care of Loo, and she could give him his Elder lessons, and then maybe life could continue as usual, just with ten on the island instead of nine. Jinny would stay, and Ess would be happy, and then, *if* she felt like it, maybe she would go off in the boat. Someday, when Ess was older. When they were both ready.

Things always feel better in the daylight, Jinny thought, and turned over to try and sleep a little more. But when she did, she heard a rustle from beneath her shifting cushions and remembered. The letter. How could she have forgotten? Jinny wriggled her hand under the makeshift bed for the envelope, slid the single sheet of paper free, unfolded it, and held it up.

In the morning light, she could see that the paper was not

white exactly but a faded yellow, and so thin as to be nearly translucent, like the wings of a dragonfly. The flowers in the corners of the page were pink, with green tendrils and leaves. At the top of the page, in pale curly letters, were the words *Abigail Ellis*.

Jinny gasped and sat up sharply. *Abigail*. She glanced briefly at the kids in the bed to be sure they were sound asleep, and then she allowed herself to read the whispery words, faded letters in a neat hand.

In all her life, until this day, Jinny had never seen a letter, but she knew about them from books. People in books were always getting letters, but this was much more exciting than the usual letter. It was a letter from a ghost, from the past. Almost as though Abigail were speaking to her, only her, from long ago and far away. The envelope had been sealed. Nobody else had ever seen this before.

Jinny read:

Dear Mom,

Geoffrey has promised to bring you this note. I hope you won't be too mad at me. I know we aren't supposed to do that-write home. That we're supposed to be really GONE while we're here. That we're supposed to try and forget you. But when I made the promise, when I agreed to come to the island, I didn't know how it would really be. I didn't know how much I'd miss you.

I miss so many things, Mommaloo! Movies. And school. And playing soccer. I miss spaghetti! It didn't occur to me there wouldn't be spaghetti here. I'm so so tired of fish. It's good fish the way Geoff makes it, with lemons from our tree, but still, when I get back I'm going to eat and eat spaghetti. Buckets of it. I almost can't remember what it feels like to be full the way spaghetti makes you full. Nuts and berries (we call them swinks, the green berries) don't fill me up like that.

I don't understand why we're here. I don't understand what this is all for. Nobody explained anything, really. Did they? Or was I not paying attention? I know sometimes I don't pay attention. It sounded like this would be summer camp when you all told us about it. But it isn't. It's days and months and years, and the adventure is gone now, and it feels like forever. Can you remind me why we're doing this? It's hard not to feel lonely sometimes, and sad.

When you get this letter, will you please send the boat back for me? I'm going a little bit crazy. I've read all the books on my shelf. I've climbed the cliffs a jillion times. I've seen all there is to see, and I'm bored, Mom. I'm ready to come home. I don't know if I can make it another whole year, until it's my turn. Maybe someone else could take my place? Maybe someone else wants to come?

I miss you so much. This will be my only letter, I promise. We've used up all our paper playing hangman, and my pencil is down to a nub. But I write you letters all the time in my head. I love you like crazy.

Sincerely, forever, your daughter (remember me?),

Abbie

Jinny read the letter. She read it again, trying to process all she'd just learned. She read it a third time.

So Abigail was really Abbie. "Abbie?" whispered Jinny. And she had a mama, a mother. A *mommaloo*? Unlike anyone else Jinny had ever known, Abigail clearly *knew* her mother. She remembered her mother. Enough to write to her this way and ask to come home. Which meant that Abigail . . . wasn't an orphan.

Jinny felt like she couldn't quite process that. Like her brain was still half asleep. She scanned the letter one more time and then clutched it to her chest as she closed her eyes. She suddenly had so many more questions. Why *hadn't* the letter gone home with Geoffrey, whoever he was? And why had Abigail—*Abbie*—if she had a mother alive, been sent to the island in the first place? Based on all the books Jinny had read, it wasn't what mothers were supposed to do—send their kids away, abandon them to live on an island. What had Abigail done to deserve that?

Jinny looked around the room, wishing there was someone

she could talk to *right now*. She opened her mouth, but no sound came out. There was nothing to say, and the littles were sleeping, but, oh, how she wanted to say *something* to *someone*. She felt like she would explode if she didn't. This was a new kind of feeling. A question bigger than a question. A mystery. A hunger, burning slowly. There was something Jinny didn't understand, and she wasn't sure what to do about it. There was so much she didn't know.

"Lemons," she whispered to herself. "What happened to the lemons?"

Jinny looked down at the letter, trembling in her tired hand. It *looked* sweet, with its flowers, but it wasn't. This letter was powerful, dangerous. Jinny could just imagine Eevie's quick fury, if she thought she had a mother who'd sent her away. Joon would pretend not to care, but her eyes would grow stormy. Nat and Ben would just be sad. They didn't get angry, only disappointed. So who could Jinny share this with? If Deen were still here, she'd show him the letter—just him—and it would be their secret. They'd fight about it, talk about it. But Deen was gone. So for now, the letter would be Jinny's. Alone.

Maybe, in his new life, Deen already had the answers to all Jinny's questions. Maybe Deen had a mother of his own and had met her. A mother like the mothers in the books. Who baked cakes, wore a bonnet, and sang him songs at night. Had she explained everything to him? Had he forgiven her?

Jinny folded the letter and looked around for a place to put it. She'd never had a thing to hide before, so she didn't have a hiding place. At last she slid it inside one of the rips in a couch cushion for safekeeping. "You'll be safe here, Abbie," she whispered to the letter, and it was oddly comforting.

After that, Jinny stacked her cushions beneath the bed and, checking to be sure that Ess and Loo were still sleeping, tip-toed outside to stretch and see what was going on. She needed to move, to run or jump. The secret inside her didn't want to sit still.

But as she was turning to walk down the path, she heard a creaking sound from the cabin next door. It was Sam. "Jinny?" he called out after her.

"Oh, hey," said Jinny, glancing over her shoulder at him quickly. He had a funny look on his face, and that made her nervous. She had the oddest sense that people might be able to *see* her secret. "What's up?"

"I just, I wanted to tell you, last night, that I think it's nice. That you stayed, for Ess."

"Oh!" said Jinny. "Wow, thank you, Sam."

"And I wish . . . Deen had done that too—stayed. I remember how you asked him, that day. And I remember how much fun we used to have, the three of us, together. It was nice, wasn't it, when we were a team, you, me, and Deen? I miss it. I still wish he hadn't left."

Jinny stared at Sam's wrinkled brow and smiled. "Sure,"

she said. It was funny to think that he remembered their trio that way. "Sure, it was great," Jinny lied kindly. "But, you know, I thought Deen seemed funny, at the end. Unhappy. Did you notice that too? Maybe he needed to go away."

Sam nodded. "He was sad. He was having scary dreams, I think. He cried in his sleep. He shouted, sometimes. It woke me up."

"Really?" It occurred to Jinny for the first time that Sam might know things about Deen that she didn't. The thought made her sad, but not as sad as she might have expected. Mostly sad for Sam. He seemed so alone with himself, so often.

"Yes," said Sam. "And also, before he left, he did this." He pointed at the ground near the cabin door.

"Did what?" asked Jinny, walking over and crouching down to inspect a line of smooth round pebbles at Sam's feet. They were fitted together perfectly, side by side, a long row of pebbles at the base of the cabin. How had she missed this? How had Deen done this without her noticing? "Huh," she said.

"Isn't it neat?" asked Sam. "Each day he found a stone, I guess, and then each night, after he tucked me in, he'd come out here and put it in the line, alone. I asked him why, and he said he couldn't explain it. He only knew that he wanted to add a stone each day."

"Hmm," said Jinny.

"I wish he hadn't gone."

"Me too." Jinny continued to stare at the stones. "But he said he had to."

"But you didn't leave Ess. So then maybe he didn't really have to leave either."

Jinny shrugged. "I'm me and Deen is Deen. But it's nice, Sam. That you remember Deen so well. That you care."

"How could I not remember him?" asked Sam. "I'll always remember him."

Jinny didn't know how to answer that, so she forced a smile, waved, turned, and started off down the path to the kitchen.

Ben didn't notice her until she was standing right behind him. She tapped him on the shoulder, and he jumped. "Oh! Jinny! I didn't see you there."

"I'm sorry," said Jinny right away.

"It's okay," Ben said. "You just gave me a startle."

"No, I mean, I'm *sorry* sorry," said Jinny. "*Really* sorry. Sorry for what happened last night."

"Oh," said Ben. "That."

"Yeah, that."

Ben looked at her without speaking. It made Jinny squirm a little. She wondered what he was thinking.

At last he said, "Well, thank you. For the apology."

Nobody said anything for another minute after that, and the silence felt stifling, so Jinny opened her mouth to fill it up, and as usual, too many words tumbled out. "Look, Ben,

I won't lie," she said. "I'd do it again, the not-leaving part. I wasn't ready to go, and I'm still not. Ess wasn't ready either. She needs me, and I—well, I'm just not ready."

"O-okay," said Ben, looking unsure.

"But about Loo . . . ," Jinny continued, "I feel terrible. I don't even know why I did that, took charge of him like I did. You're right, of course. I didn't think of you, or anyone else, and I'm sorry I upset you and made things hard. I didn't want to upset you. I just wanted to stay. *Here*."

Ben stared at her evenly. There was a spoon in his hand, and he glanced down at the spoon, then back at Jinny, before he said, "I won't lie either, Jinny. I think you're wrong to do this. All of it. I think you should get into that boat today and go. Right now. Because these are the only rules we have, and it's good here, when we follow them. Or it always has been, so far. But for your sake, I hope it will all be fine. And I *do* understand. At least, I *mostly* understand. Does that make sense?"

"Yes, I think so," said Jinny, searching his face, trying to see whether this meant she was forgiven. She still wasn't sure.

"Well," said Ben. "All right." Then he smiled, and Jinny felt a tiny gust of relief. Ben was smiling.

"Hey," said Jinny more brightly. "So, then . . . about Loo. I decided you can have him. You can be Elder now. It's okay with me. I'll just keep Ess."

Still frowning slightly, Ben slapped the spoon against his

hand softly. "No, I think . . . No."

"What do you mean?" asked Jinny. "It's what you wanted. I'm trying to make things right."

"And I accept your apology," agreed Ben. "But that doesn't change the fact that you made a choice, and now Loo thinks you're his Elder, and honestly I just want to stay out of this mess. You can be in charge. Of everything."

Jinny blinked in surprise. "Are you sure?"

Ben nodded at her. "I'm sure. And you were right about one thing. I have plenty to do here, without a Care." Then he smiled again cautiously and turned back to his cooking, before adding, "Besides, he looks like you, you know. Loo."

"He does?" Jinny was startled by the thought. Really, she had no idea what she looked like. But it was funny to think she looked like the new little boy.

Ben nodded. "Sure. He has your eyes."

"Oh, yeah," said Jinny. "That . . ."

"Other things too," said Ben. "He reminds me of you in other ways."

"Really?" Jinny wasn't sure what that meant or if she liked it.

But Ben didn't answer again. Something was bubbling on the stove that seemed to need his attention, so Jinny escaped and ran nimbly up the path, to start fresh.

As she ran, a memory followed her up the hill. *Blue eyes*. Her own blue eyes. She'd been on the island for several years before anyone had bothered to inform her that her eyes were blue. She'd always assumed they were brown. Maybe light brown, like Tate's, or nearly black, like Deen's. But everyone had brown eyes, so of course she'd assumed the same about her own. It had been Deen who'd corrected her one day. "Blue, you big goof!" he'd said with a laugh. "Your eyes are blue, Jinny."

"What? That's ridiculous," she'd argued. "Who has blue eyes? Only people in books." She'd thought he was playing a trick on her.

"People in books, and you," Deen had insisted.

"Really? Blue?"

Deen had nodded. "Just like the sky," he'd said pointing upward. "Like *that*."

Soon, Jinny was back at her cabin. She opened the door with a bang.

"Ess," she sang, tousling the girl's hair in the usual way. "Time to get up."

"I'm up!" sang Ess, sitting up straight, but with her eyes still closed.

Jinny leaned in to wake Loo. She poked him in the belly with a soft finger. "Loo," she said gently. "Hey, you, Loo! Good morning, and welcome!"

Loo didn't wake up.

Ess tried next. She leaned in past Jinny and shouted. "Loo, get up! It's breakfast time!"

Loo didn't say a word, but he did answer Ess, in a way. Though his eyes never opened, a little arm shot out, with a balled-up fist at the end of it, and punched her in the chin.

"Ow!" cried Ess,falling back on the bed.

"Loo!" shouted Jinny.

"Whah?" said Loo, sitting up, and looking at Jinny wide-eyed. With those big startling blue eyes trained on her blankly. Like he had no idea what he'd done.

Or almost like that.

17

Getting to Know Loo

From that moment forward, Loo was a lot of work. Perhaps, Jinny thought, as she chased him down the path to the fire circle, he was just too tired last night to get into trouble. But now he was rested, and he seemed to be making up for lost time. In a funny way, Jinny was glad for the distraction. Nobody had a chance to be resentful of her at breakfast. Not with Loo shouting and slurping and smacking his plate on the table.

Whereas Jinny remembered both Ess and Sam as timid and watchful on their first morning, Loo was the opposite—all sound and movement, like a thigh-high thunderstorm. He shouted and demanded. He jumped and hopped. He had trouble sitting still, and he did *not* like eggs, and he did *not* want nutcakes either, and he liked to throw the things he didn't like, to be sure everyone knew. But he was still *VEWWY HUNGWY.*

"How about some fish cake?" tried Jinny with a sigh.

Loo made a face and shouted, "No! No! No!"

Jinny, exasperated, turned to Ben for help. "I don't know what else to try. I wasn't aware that there were people who didn't like any kind of food at all ever."

Ben shrugged, unfazed. "Remember when Sam got here? He didn't eat for two days. It drove Deen crazy."

"I don't remember that, actually," said Jinny, wondering how she'd missed noticing. "But I'm guessing Sam didn't shout and scream either." She glanced over at Sam, who was quietly cleaning his plate.

"No, I don't know that I've ever heard Sam shout, come to think of it," said Ben. "Not even that time Oz whacked him in the eye with a stick." Just then Loo let out a wild wail. Ben glanced at the boy briefly, then back at Jinny. "Well," he added pleasantly, "good luck with him!"

Jinny frowned at Ben. "Boo," she said. But it was a relief, to see that Ben seemed like he'd truly forgiven her. Anyway, he was acting like himself again. She turned back to Loo and tried again. "How about some dried snaps?" She reached for a handful and held them out.

Loo scowled and shook his head. "Bech!" he said, slapping her hand away.

At last, Loo was talked into eating a bowl of leftover stewed plomms, though most of the fruit seemed to end up on his face.

After breakfast, Loo hopped down right away and began to point at things. All the things. He wanted to know what *this* was and what *that* was, and he wanted to touch the fire circle, and he wanted to run into the water. "Now!" he demanded, pointing. "Now, now, now!"

It seemed like every other minute someone was shouting out, "No, Loo, NO!"

At last, to give the others a chance to clean up and catch their breaths, Jinny decided to take Loo to lose his shoes. "Come on!" she said, reaching out one hand to him and another to Ess. "I'm going to show you something neat. Okay?" Loo ignored her hand and instead catapulted himself off toward the beach and ran ahead. Ess followed him, and Jinny sighed, watching them run.

"Feel free to take your time," Joon said to Jinny. "Feel free to stay all day." As Jinny headed off after her Cares, Joon added, "Wow! That new kid is more trouble than Oz and Jak put together."

Oz grinned. "No kidding! I guess we need to work a little harder, huh, Jak? Loo is a total disaster!"

Jinny turned and called back at them over her shoulder. "You know, I can still hear you!" she shouted. The others only laughed.

Following Ess and Loo as they took off down the beach,

Jinny found herself thinking about how tall Ess seemed now, compared to this new little boy, how much she'd grown. And it wasn't just her height. Ess walked calmly down the beach, while Loo was in constant motion. Jumping and shouting. Zigging and zagging. Periodically racing forward with a sudden burst of speed for no clear reason. He was chaos.

But as hard as it was to keep up with him, Jinny had to admire Loo. He was agile, like a wild animal, spry and darting, quick and confident in his steps. Where Ess had always been ungainly, tripping over the air and toppling when she ran, Loo was strong, surefooted. When he came to a huge tortoise in the sand, he sprang over it and cleared the creature, almost without noticing it was a living thing. Ess stumbled along behind him, then stopped to tap on its shell and say hello.

When they reached the bone tree and the shoe pile, Loo had no trouble whatsoever giving up his shoes. Jinny tried to explain to him what was happening. She wanted him to understand the importance of the pile. Ess wanted to show him her bracelet, her *mama*, and point out her own shoes, which she sometimes liked to visit. But Loo wasn't interested in listening. Instead, he began scrambling in the sandy pile. Digging and curious, crowing at the tiny scuttles and sand beetles living in the old shoes. When he smashed a scuttle between two fingers, Jinny thought Ess was going to cry.

Then he began to dismantle the pile. "Hey, whoa, Loo!" Jinny cried as he tossed the faded shoes into the air all around him. "Stop! You're messing it all up. We don't do that. We leave these shoes alone. This place is . . . special. It's been like this for as long as we've been on the island. It's our job to take care of it, to watch over it. We're responsible for it. Do you understand?"

Loo clearly heard Jinny's words, but he said nothing in reply. Then he whirled back around and continued to throw the shoes as far as he could. Meanwhile, Ess scurried to recover her own canvas sneakers. She found one a few feet away from the pile, and immediately began to hunt around for its mate.

In a matter of moments all the shoes were dispersed, and Loo began to dig in the sand with his hands. Jinny stared at his back, unsure of what to do next. She was having a hard time knowing how much Loo was in control of his actions, and how much he was just very, very young. But at least he was occupied now. Jinny sighed and turned to clean up the shoes. She would need to reconstruct the pile. Ess was one step ahead of her, helping without being asked. She'd already started collecting the shoes in pairs, and then lining them up so that the pairs of shoes made a sort of parade in the sand, along the waterline.

It was interesting, Jinny thought, as she walked along and stared at Ess's line, how the shoes differed as much as Ess and Loo did. Some of them were made of cloth and rubber, and many of them had a funny strip of plastic bristles to fasten them. Others were leather, with rusted buckles or rotted laces.

She reached down to pick up one particular shoe and found it was bigger than most of them. Slim and flat and made of leather, with no fasteners of any kind. In fact . . . Jinny leaned over and fitted the old slipper onto her own callused foot, and it slid on just so. It fit perfectly, snug and stiff.

For some reason, gazing at all the matched pairs of shoes, Jinny began to count them. One. Two. Three pairs. Jinny counted them all. Forty pairs. Eighty shoes, each with a match. Not a single one missing in all those years. And now that she was looking at them, she noticed that only a few pairs were larger than the others, like the slipper on her foot—but only a few. Why was that?

Jinny stared at all the shoes. Deen's must be here, somewhere. She tried to imagine Deen small enough for the tiny shoes, and found it made her smile to picture him so young. She couldn't remember him little, could only imagine his older face—sharp cheekbones framed by floppy hair—atop a compact little body like Loo's.

Idly, Jinny wondered if perhaps a pair of the bigger shoes had belonged to Abigail. "Abbie," she corrected herself, in a whisper. Based on the letter, Abbie had come to the island when she was older. She couldn't have come here when she was Loo's age, or she wouldn't remember her *mommaloo* so well or be able to write so prettily. Jinny considered her foot in the cracked slipper. This might even be Abbie's shoe, on her very own foot. She hunted around and found the mate, slid it on. It felt odd to be wearing shoes. Tight. A new feeling. The soles were cracked and scratchy. Her feet looked like someone else's. Like feet from a picture in a book. Alice's feet. Or Dorothy's. Feet from the world out *there*. Did nobody ever wiggle their toes out there? Did they all dress in things so stiff? Jinny took off the shoes.

Heading back up the beach to join the others a little while later, Loo and Ess ran ahead of Jinny. Loo leaped up onto a dune, and then the air filled with shrieking, as the boy began to scream wildly, kicking his legs in front of him, punching the air. A few feet away, Ess was standing statue still. Frozen.

Jinny sprinted up to them. "What is it? What's wrong?" She reached for Loo, who was still screaming, but he didn't stop. She lifted his writhing, shouting body off the ground, but he was wild, strong, all clenched muscles, and hard to hold. "Shhh!" said Jinny. Then Loo pointed and Jinny saw what had scared him. A snake. Coiled in the sand, blocking his way.

"Oh," laughed Jinny. "That. Don't worry. It's just a snake. No need to shout." She set the boy back down in the sand. Immediately, he wrapped his arms around her waist, whimpering to be carried.

"Loo," hushed Jinny. "Loo, Loo, Loo . . . calm down. It's nothing. Animals are our friends, when they aren't our dinner. There's nothing to shout about. Here on the island all the animals are safe. Look at Ess. See, she's not scared. She loves the snakes. Right, Ess?"

But when Jinny looked over, Ess was in fact standing rigid, with her arms frozen at her sides. Her eyes were wide, and she didn't even turn to look at Jinny. She looked as scared as Loo, only quieter.

Dragging Loo with her, because his arms were still connected to her hips, Jinny walked the three long paces in the sand, to lean over Ess. "Ess, what is it? What's wrong? You know better. It's only a snakey. It's nothing. It's fine."

Ess looked up at Jinny through tears. "It hissed," Ess said. "That snake hissed. At me, and he showed me his teeth. He's a mean snake. Mean. Look, Jinny." She raised a stiff arm and pointed.

Jinny smiled reassuringly, but when her eyes fell on the snake, she saw something she'd never seen before. The snake *wasn't* lying in the sand, basking in the sun, like usual. Instead it had raised its head up high, nearly a foot in the air, and was staring at them, its tongue flicking in and out, its eyes level and staring, straight at them.

"Ooh, it does look a little scary, doesn't it?" said Jinny, feeling slightly unnerved herself. "Standing up like that? I see what you mean. That *is* odd. But he's still just a snake. Okay? Snakes don't bite. That only happens in stories. Our snakes are nice snakes."

Ess shook her head. "I think he's a mean snake."

Loo bellowed, "MEAN SNAKE!" at the top of his lungs.

"No, no. It's fine, I promise," said Jinny. "Now hush, no need to yell."

But even as she shushed her Cares, Jinny had to admit that something about the rigid snake scared her too. The tongue flickering like a warning, the black eyes watching her so carefully. Jinny wondered why she'd never seen such a thing until now. Something about it made her want to hold Ess tight.

Just then, Loo gave a shriek, let go of Jinny's waist, and bolted. He ran away from her, away from the snake, away from the water, farther up and over the dunes. Jinny sighed and turned to follow, dragging Ess behind.

18

Strange Catch

A few days later, bright and early, everyone on the island was roused by shouting. They all burst from their sleeping cabins and dashed for the cove, but halted on the path when it became clear that the shouting was only excitement. Down by the water, Jak and Oz were whooping into their nets.

"What is it?" Joon called out from her spot on the ridge. She peered down at the boys on the dock. "What's happening? Is everyone all right?"

"Just fine," bellowed Oz in reply. He looked back up at the cabins, squinting in the hazy sunrise. "Better than fine. We've got an inkfish!"

Joon flashed a quick grin. "For true?"

"Yeah, inkfish!" said Jak, jumping uncontrollably up and down on the dock.

Sam, Ess, and Loo looked baffled by all this. But the older kids were grinning broadly, from one to the other. Inkfish!

"Come on, guys, hurry!" Jinny urged her Cares, shoving them back up the path and inside the cabin to dress.

Sam looked lost in the shuffle, still standing in his cabin doorway alone. "Inkfish?" he asked. "What's an inkfish? Deen didn't tell me about inkfish."

"Get dressed!" said Ben, running past. "You'll see!"

A few minutes later all the kids stood on the beach and watched as Oz and Jak attempted to haul a huge slippery creature from the dock to the kitchen in a bucket several sizes too small.

"Oh!" said Sam, when he caught sight of the strange beast, its many legs dragging in the sand.

"Bech!" shouted Loo. "Icky!"

"What's it?" asked Ess. "Jinny, what's a ninkfish?"

"Fun!" said Jinny. "An inkfish is wonderful fun!" She tried to ignore Loo's noises of disgust and turned away from him to grin at Ess. "It's going to be a good time. Just you wait!"

Once the animal was up on the table, they all gazed in awe. It was enormous, as big as Loo, stretched out, so that its many strange slimy legs draped and fell over the rough board surface into the sand. The inkfish was a funny color, a sort of purple-pink, with black dots all over. Loo ran forward to poke at it with a finger, and nobody stopped him. They all wanted to see what would happen. Nothing did.

"Has anyone ever actually seen one before?" asked Nat thoughtfully. "Or have we all just heard the stories?"

"I have," offered Ben. "I was little. I think I was still a Care. But I remember. That means Jinny remembers too, right, Jinny?"

Jinny nodded. "Yes," she said foggily, barely recalling it, the last inkfish. It had been an event. "But that was a long time ago."

"Why is it so good?" asked Sam. "What does it do?"

"It's not what it does," said Jinny. "It's what you can do with it."

"Well," said Oz, bouncing slightly on his toes, "do it. Make it happen! Cut it open!" He looked to Ben, who generally wielded the knives in the kitchen.

Ben considered the slimy, confusing creature on the table, and then he looked at Jinny and grinned. "I think Jinny should do it," he said. "After all, she's the Elder, right? She's in charge. She should have the honor."

"What, me?" asked Jinny. "No way. You should. I mean, you're much better at stuff like that."

"Truth is," confessed Ben, "I have no clue what to do, and I don't want to ruin it."

"Well, gosh, me neither," said Jinny.

"Well, someone has to do it," said Oz. "Someone give me

a knife. I'll cut that sucker open right now!"

With an exasperated sigh, Joon tossed both hands into the air. "You're all ridiculous. Here, let me." She reached down to the table, grabbed the knife, and then, as everyone watched, plunged it deep into the thick, meaty head of the inkfish. Then she drew a huge jagged tear through the flesh, which gave way easily. She stepped back. "I hope I didn't do it wrong. Ben, you look and see."

Ben reached in, lifted the flap of flesh, and stuck a hand inside the creature. He rooted around, searching for something. "I think . . . *this* is it," he said with a sigh of relief. "It feels fine. Hand me the small knife." Then, delicately, he cut into the fish and extracted a blobby sort of sack. Carefully he pulled it free, then laid it on the table beside the carcass. "There!" he said. "It's real and full. Ink!"

"Ink!" chorused the others.

"Someone else collect feathers and twigs. We'll get rocks!" said Oz excitedly, already running in the direction of the tide pools. "C'mon, Jak! Let's go!"

While the littles ran to find feathers on the beach, Ben carried away the strange fish and then scrubbed the table down. In no time at all they'd gathered back at the same spot, where Ben set out the ink, portioned into several small bowls. Then Oz and Jak returned, lugging a bag of smooth white stones from the tide pools, and passed them around so that each had a rock to paint on.

Jinny stared at her stone for a moment, and then up at the sky, trying to think what to draw. There was nothing else on the island like this. No way to make a mark. They all carved pictures with sticks in the wet sand now and then, but the tides or the night rain inevitably came to wash those away. Sometimes the kids drew with charred sticks on the sides of their cabins, but that too wore off. Or they carved with a knife, but crudely. Swink juice faded and ran. Only this—inkfish ink—had ever lasted. Jinny wasn't sure what had happened to her rock from when she was little, but there were a few stones, on a high shelf in the book cabin, painted with flowers and stars.

"Just think," said Nat, staring at the flat white surface of her stone. "This will *last*. What we do now might still be here years from now. Isn't that strange?"

"Yes, even after we're gone," said Ben, eyes on his rock.

"Yeah," said Jinny, glancing his way. "After that."

Ben looked up. "Okay, guys, be sparing with the ink, so everyone gets enough. *Share*. But don't take too long either, or it might all dry all up." He dipped his feather gently into the bowl before him. Then he grinned. "Here we go!"

Jinny held her feather lightly in her hand. Beside her on each side, both Ess and Loo were already scribbling and blobbing ink all over their stones. That was fine. They were having fun.

Jinny wasn't sure what to draw. At last, she wrote her name, *JINNY*. It looked funny. She wasn't used to seeing it written out like that. After another moment, she drew a looping line all around the word, a frame. She meant it to look like the morning sky, with all its whorls and swirls. But the brownish-black line on the white stone didn't look like the vivid bursting sky at all. When Jinny tried to wipe it clean and start over, it only smudged, as the ink bled into the tiny cracks in the rock. That was no good. Jinny wanted to make something special, something worthy of the ink. She might never get another chance at this, ever. She pouted and turned her stone over. She ran her hand softly over the fresh new surface, so smooth and clean. What to draw?

Then she noticed that both Joon and Ben had stopped painting to stare at the other end of the table, where Nat was working in utter silence and concentration. Her tongue was clenched between her teeth, and her eyes were fixed on the surface before her. No part of her body seemed to be moving except her fingers, which clutched her feather tight and low, just above the inky point. Her fingertips were brown, but she didn't seem to have noticed.

Jinny stood up so that she could lean in and see what Nat was painting, what the others were looking at. When she did, she gasped. "Oh, *Nat*!"

There was a face, a set of eyes staring out of the stone. But it wasn't a face Jinny had ever seen before. It wasn't a child's face. It was a strange face, unfamiliar, haunting. The face was lined and creased, with circles under its eyes. The face looked tired but happy. Wisps of hair framed it and looked to be in motion, caught in an imaginary breath of wind. The face looked old. Like a witch from a book. But loving.

Even in brown and white, even on the hard cold stone, the face looked real. Nearly alive, as though it might speak to them all if they were quiet enough. Jinny watched intently as Nat leaned back, looking thoughtfully at her picture, then licked a fingertip and smudged at the stone in a way that shaded the face, made it appear even more alive.

"Wow," said Joon, peering down over Nat's shoulder. "That's amazing, Nat. How did you know how to do that?"

Nat didn't seem to hear her. Or anyway, she didn't answer. She was still staring at her artwork, lost in her picture. At last, she looked up, and her tongue slipped from between her teeth. She glanced around at all her friends, as though she'd had no idea they were looking at her. "What?" she asked. "Why are you all staring?"

"Because you just made *that*," said Eevie. "And we made junk like *this*." She held up her own stone, which had a crude tree drawn on it. A series of lines connected to one another in a rough way. "We're jealous."

"I'm not jealous," said Ben, shaking his head. "I'm just amazed. It's really something special, Nat. A kind of magic. Inside you."

"Yeah, wow," said Jak, awestruck.

And for once Oz echoed *him*, nodding. "Wow."

"Who is it?" asked Jinny. "That face? Who did you paint?"

Nat looked down at the stone and scratched her nose. When she did, she left a brownish-black smudge there, right on the tip. "I don't know," she said. "I didn't think about it. I just painted what came to me, what was in my head. I guess maybe that's who lives in my head? Maybe it's someone I remember. A face from . . . before?" Nat looked around at them all, as bewildered by what she'd made as anyone.

"It looks like a mama," said Ess, nodding. "No, a gramma."

Jinny blinked in surprise. It had been so many sleeps since *mama* had meant anything to Ess but her bracelet. But she didn't look upset. She seemed okay, so Jinny said nothing about it.

After that they went back to their own attempts at painting flowers, dots, and in the case of Loo, a big blodgy handprint. None of them were memorable, though everyone had a fine time.

Jinny watched Nat a little longer, thinking about the people who lived in her own head, and wishing she could make something so lovely. There *was* a face she'd paint, if she could. A face she'd like to be able to see peering out from a stone on her windowsill. Finally, she picked up her feather and made four more letters. Below her own name she wrote another word.

Deen.

When Jinny sat back, she saw that Sam was staring across the table at her stone. He read the upside-down name, his lips moving slowly. Then he looked up at her, and Jinny thought he might be about to cry. But before she could say anything, he gave a sniff and glanced back at his rock. Jinny felt a twinge of guilt. Sam was so easy to ignore, so quiet. On his stone was a picture of a fish. Just a regular old fish. Jinny wondered why he'd chosen to draw a fish.

She stared at him working, head down, with his hair flopped over his face, and remembered Deen carrying the boy on his tall shoulders, too tired to walk home from a fetch. Sam had fallen asleep in just that same position, hair in face, without anyone realizing it, until he gave a loud snore and woke himself up. They'd laughed at the time. *I remember how much fun we used to have, the three of us together*, Sam had said. Maybe he wasn't as sad as Jinny thought he was. Maybe he just *seemed* sad.

But Jinny had plenty to think about without puzzling out Sam. Too much, really. And Sam wasn't her job. It was Deen who'd owed him something—more than a sudden departure, at any rate. It was Deen who had left him. She glanced down the table at Ess, drawing flowers, and felt fiercely glad. I stayed, she thought. I did it. And I'm not ashamed of that. The others can be mad, but it's a good thing. Everyone else lets go—Tate, Deen . . . whoever sent us here. But not me.

After a while, the ink began to dry, leaving brown rings in the bottoms of their pewter bowls, and it was time to clean up. One by one the kids left the table and carried their stones off to their sleeping cabins. The stones would last. That was the main thing about stones and ink—they lasted.

Jinny sat longer at the table than anyone else, watching the others leave. When they were gone, she picked up her feather and the last dish of ink, almost gone now. But instead of walking down to the water to rinse the bowl, she had a thought. She looked around and took note of Ess and Loo, playing on the beach with Nat. Safe with Nat. Clutching her stone and the bowl, Jinny left the table and sprinted up the sandy path to her own cabin.

When she got to her room, Jinny shut the door carefully, and—moving as quickly as she could, because someone might always come knocking—she pulled the letter from Abbie through the rip in its cushion. She turned it over and ran her finger across the pale yellow back of the paper, the empty expanse. Then Jinny spit into the ink bowl to rewet it, dipped her feather in, and wrote.

Dear reader . . .

Jinny stopped then and sat, trying to think. Distantly, she heard the cries of the other kids from the beach. She looked back down at the sheet of paper, dipped her pen again, and continued.

Dear reader who finds this, if I am gone,
My name is Jinny.

I lived here on this island.

I loved it.

I stayed.

I held on.

Jinny stopped writing again and stared down at the words, *her* words. They didn't seem like very much. They didn't seem to say anything at all, really. But they were the words she wanted to put down on the page. Her vision suddenly blurred. Why on earth was she crying? "It doesn't matter what I write," she said to herself. "The thing is to have written *something*."

When she was finished, Jinny looked back at what she'd made, tried to imagine what it would look like to the kid who found it. Her letters were nothing like Abbie's loopy, pretty writing. They were shaky, and the inkfish ink was uneven, drying in scratches and clumps. But it was still a letter, a real letter. She'd written it.

Once the ink was dry, Jinny folded the letter in half and slipped it back into her cushion. Maybe *someone* would find it someday, the way she'd found Abbie's letter.

Even if nobody ever found it, Jinny had left it behind.

19

A Funny Coincidence

That night for dinner, Ben set out several different platters of food, none of them exactly full. In the center was the grilled inkfish, its tentacles curling crisply. As he arranged them on the table, he called out to nobody and everybody, "Hey, you guys should probably start helping more, with the meals, from now on."

"Why should we?" asked Eevie, arriving at the table. When she saw the inkfish, she wrinkled her nose and added, "Ew! We aren't really going to eat that, are we?"

"It's what we have, so it's what we'll eat," said Ben. "And you need to learn to cook because it's something everyone needs to know how to do."

"We all know how to cook," said Eevie.

"Sort of," admitted Jak. "We wouldn't starve."

"Well, you need to know more. Because I won't always be here to do it for you."

"You won't? Really?" asked Joon, who had just walked up. "When do you plan to go?" She looked down the beach in the direction of the green boat.

"Oh, I don't mean *that*," said Ben. "I mean, no particular time. Just . . . maybe, someday." He glanced at Jinny, who busied herself with sitting down at the table, reaching for a plate, looking the other way.

Jinny didn't know what to think about this conversation. It made her feel itchy, because it was about her, and it wasn't. Jinny didn't want to leave the island herself, but for some reason, she didn't want anyone else to take her place either. And with the green boat sitting up on the sand like that, it was true that anyone could go, at any time. Jinny hadn't thought about that before, and she was pondering it when Loo, beside her, began to bash his spoon against his metal plate for no apparent reason.

"Jeez!" Jinny was suddenly pulled from her thoughts. "What is it now?" she shouted, whirling around and facing him.

Standing on the other side of Loo, Joon shot Jinny a critical glance, then leaned over to help the boy. "Hey, look," she said, pointing to all the different bowls and plates. "So many things to choose from for supper. What would you like?"

Loo only pointed at the inkfish, stuck out his tongue, and made a retching sound. When Joon looked disgusted, Jinny couldn't help smiling to herself. See, Joon, she thought. Not so easy.

Oz, surveying the table, managed to keep his tongue in his mouth, but he didn't look exactly pleased either. "What's this all about?" he said, pointing at the little bowls. "Besides the inkfish, there's just scraps here."

"Yeah," echoed Jak. "What's this all about?"

Ben shrugged. "I'm not sure why, but we had nothing in the nets this morning except the inkfish, and the chickens aren't laying well. It's weird that both happened at the same time."

A funny coincidence, thought Jinny. She picked a splinter from the rough wood of the table and said nothing.

Ben continued. "Since we didn't have quite enough of anything to make a proper meal, I just cooked up all that was left in the kitchen. Everyone can eat whatever they like best, and then we can all go on a big fetch tomorrow. How does that sound?"

"Can we go for honey?" asked Nat. "We've been out of honey for so many sleeps I can't even remember what it tastes like."

"Certainly," said Ben, sitting down and reaching for the leftover mussels. Everyone else took that as a cue to begin the meal, and they all found something to eat, even if it wasn't quite enough.

Loo, however, was not pleased with the arrangement. "Loo want pomms," he said. "More pomms. Pomms, pomms, pomms!"

"Ugh," grumbled Eevie. "Can someone please shut him up?"

Jinny opened her mouth to respond, but after their last horrible fight, Jinny didn't want to start another. She ignored Eevie for once, and turned to Loo. "Here you go," she said, setting a wedge of fruit on his plate. "You can have the last plomm."

Loo poked at the unfamiliar object on his plate. "Pomm?"

"It's not stewed," said Jinny. "But it tastes the same, I promise. Now eat."

Loo looked up at Jinny and scowled, as though he wasn't convinced. But he ran his finger over the fruit, licked the finger, and decided it would do. He picked up the half plomm in both hands and buried his face in it. Which meant that however big a mess he was making, at least he was no longer chanting.

Jinny felt a tug on her sleeve. When she turned around, she found that Ess was pouting up at her.

"Not you too now!" said Jinny. "What's wrong?"

Ess's voice was small when she said, "I wanted plomms. Like Loo."

"Oh . . . well, I'm sorry," said Jinny, looking at the slobbery remnant in Loo's hands. "I don't think you want to share what's left with him, do you?"

Ess shook her head slowly.

"I promise we'll pick more tomorrow, okay?" said Jinny. "In the meantime, how about some nuts?"

Ess stared at Jinny blankly.

"Ess?" Jinny said.

The girl didn't answer.

"Did you hear me, Ess? You want some nuts?"

Ess shook her head slowly. "No," she said at last. "I don't want nuts."

"No? Are you sure?"

"I'm not hungry anymore," said Ess. "Scoose me." She slid down from her bench and headed back for the sleeping cabin, her steps more determined and regular than usual. She plodded evenly and didn't trip or stumble even once.

"Ess?" Jinny called after her. "Ess, are you okay?"

Ess didn't turn. She just kept walking. Any other day Jinny would have followed, but Loo was dripping his fruit everywhere. So she reached for a rag instead and mopped his face with it.

"What's wrong with her?" asked Oz, watching Ess go.

"She said she wanted a plomm," said Jinny.

"I bet she's jealous," said Eevie in a matter-of-fact tone, taking a gulp of water.

"You always think everyone is jealous," said Joon.

"Jealous of what?" asked Oz from across the table.

"Eevie might be right this time," said Ben. "At least a little bit. I think maybe Ess is having a hard time." He motioned at Loo with a jerk of his head. "I mean, is she still even your Care now?"

Around the table the others all nodded. Loo, oblivious to the conversation, went back to shoving his face into the fruit, smacking his lips and dripping.

Jinny snapped. "Well, you guys are forever telling me I baby her, aren't you? So maybe this is a lesson she needs to learn—that I can't be in two places at once!"

"You aren't supposed to need to be in two places at once," said Ben.

Without quite meaning to, Jinny slammed down her fork. "Look, I'm doing the best I can," she said, before glancing around at everyone. "I can't make plomms appear out of thin air. And I didn't see any of you suggesting we take away Loo's plomm."

"Gosh, no," said Eevie. "We don't want to start that howling ruckus up again."

Later, banging the dishes around in the sink, Jinny tried not to think about Ess, back in the cabin, alone. It didn't work. Jinny's frustration from earlier had burned away, and now she just felt guilty, even if she didn't know what else she could have done. She scrubbed extra hard, as if to rid her thoughts of Ess, walking away from the table.

Setting aside the last plate, Jinny considered that she could probably never feel about Loo the way she did about Ess. She felt bad about that, but the boy was always moving. He never stopped shouting. He was rude and wild. At night he breathed through his mouth and it kept her awake. But still, he was her Care and he needed her. Ess would be okay. Jinny would do something special with her tomorrow to make up for it. They'd go for a walk all by themselves.

When Jinny turned from the sink, she jumped. "Ben!" she said. He was sitting at the table, watching her in silence. How long had he been waiting like that, staring at her back? "You scared me. Did you want something?"

"I just . . . thought maybe we could talk."

"About what?" asked Jinny. There was plenty to talk about, of course. But she didn't really want to get into any of it. She had enough to worry about without Ben and his feelings.

"I just wanted to see if you're okay," said Ben. "You seem upset tonight. Jumpy."

Jinny shook her head. She did feel jumpy. But where to begin, and what would be the point of talking? Anyway, how could she explain what she didn't understand herself? "No," she said. "No, I'm just busy. And tired. All this work with Ess and Loo . . . it's a lot. But please don't say I told you so. . . ."

"I wouldn't do that," said Ben. "I never would."

"Thanks," said Jinny. She tried to smile. "Look, Ben, I know you didn't agree with it, but as hard as it is, I'm glad I stayed. I truly am."

"That's good, I guess," said Ben. "I mean, I'm glad you're glad. But I just, well . . . I want to help you, if I can." He stared at her for another moment, like he was waiting for her to say something.

It was kind of him. Jinny could tell he was trying, but he wasn't really helping. "Good night, Ben," she said finally, then turned and walked away.

20

Something Stirred

Jinny woke up, stared at the wooden planks of the ceiling through half-glazed eyes, and then closed them again. "Mmm . . . ," she said. She turned over into the pillow, tried to find her way back into sleep, into her dream. Away from the hard floor and the lumpy cushions into that other place. That soft place. There.

But where was *there*? Jinny couldn't find it, the dream. She'd been so warm. Close and happy. Like there was sunshine on her, slippering her skin. Or no—had it been water? Yes. Water on sun and her beneath it all, sliding and sleeping in between the lapping waves. Water holding her.

Yes, and now she was drifting, falling back, floating, almost *there*. Swimming in the warm sunshine water. So all around her the water and the sun, like a bubble, and arms, *like water but not water*, more solid than water, enfolding her. Tight watery arms, and strong. Now Jinny wasn't slipping. She was floating, held up by the arms and the water. She was in a bubble. She was a bubble. And the arms were all around her, and Jinny was safe. While the voice was saying . . . something? What was the voice saying?

Jinny.

Jinny, sang the voice, in humming underwater tones.

But the voice was familiar. It was Deen's voice. *Jinny Jinny Jinny.*

And now the waves were Deen's arms. Deen's waves, his sunshine bubble, and Jinny couldn't hear him singing anymore, but that was okay because the arms were there, all around her.

Jinny held her breath easily. She waited. She floated. Happy.

Until . . . a breath of air, cold.

She gasped and sat up. Her bare shoulders were freezing. She glanced around the room quickly and noticed the door was open, letting in an early-morning chill. She climbed up, out of her cushions to close the door, and glanced over at the bed, where she saw only Loo, facedown in a pillow. Alone.

Alone?

Ess was gone.

Hazily, Jinny remembered dinner the night before. Then the bubble burst. The ghost of the warm dream slipped away with the cold morning breeze, and Jinny found herself hopping up and yanking Loo along with her, out of the cabin. But when they stepped out into the day, Jinny froze. Because something was different. Something big. Gazing up and out into the morning, Jinny saw that the sunrise shapes—the whorls and swirls that usually filled the sky—looked different than they ever had before. The ring of mist that surrounded the island was looser somehow, so the sunrise blurred rather than creating its usual clear pictures. There were no flowers, no fish or stars. Only a blurry, hazy scrim over the gold-and-blue sky. She squinted and peered up intently.

Dragging the sleepy boy behind her, she ran down the sandy path to the fire circle, still in her sleeping shift.

"Has anyone seen Ess?" she called out in a voice that felt raw and unready. Not yet awake. She cleared her throat. "Essssss!"

Joon, stoking the fire in the cookstove, looked over her shoulder and said, "What? No. Isn't she in your cabin?"

"Well, if she were in my cabin, I wouldn't be looking for her, now would I?" replied Jinny. She had to shout over Loo's howls. Now that he was back in the kitchen, he wanted more plomms, and of course there weren't any. "Hush!" Jinny shouted at him, and his mouth snapped shut. A miracle.

"Hey, did you guys see the sky?" asked Nat, appearing on the path. "What's going on?"

"It's weird," said Jinny. "But what's weirder is I can't find

Ess. She wasn't in the cabin when we woke up. Nobody's seen her."

"Well, to be fair, you've only asked me," said Joon. "*Somebody* may well have seen her."

"This isn't like her." Jinny could feel the worry building inside her. Loo began shouting again, hopping on one foot. Why didn't he ever shut up?

Nat smiled and raised her eyebrows at Jinny.

"What?" Jinny snapped. "Why are you smiling? There's nothing funny about this!"

Nat pointed at the table a few feet away, and when Jinny glanced down at it, she recognized a lumpy tuft of tangled black hair sticking out from under the tabletop.

"Ess!" Jinny shouted. She dashed the short distance, ducked down, and then fell over with relief. There, beneath the table, sat Ess and Sam. Both of them were grinning.

"What were you thinking?" Jinny said. "You gave me a huge fright!"

"We were hiding," said Sam shyly. "Me and Ess. Right, Ess?"

"Yes!" said Ess proudly. "Me and Sam!"

"You guys!" said Jinny, with mingled tones of annoyance and relief. "You can't run off hiding, first thing in the morning. Nobody knew where you were. I was worried. And, Sam, I know you know better than that!"

"I'm sorry," said Sam gravely. His eyes were very serious.

He wasn't accustomed to being yelled at.

"Me too," said Ess brightly, with a firm nod of her head. "But it's okay. Okay?"

Jinny groaned and stood up. "Yeah, it's okay." She walked back over to where Loo stood and reached for his hand. "Let's start this day all over again. Do-over! Come on, Loo. We need to change our clothes."

As she marched back up the path, dragging the squawking Loo behind her, Jinny found herself filled with a mix of feelings. Relief, of course. But she was surprised to discover another emotion tangled up with the relief. A faint twinge of envy. She tried to dismiss it, shrug it off, but there it was. Ess had never gone off without her before this. And Sam, of all people . . . Jinny knew it was silly and tried to shake away the feeling. But it stuck.

Then, like a flash, Jinny found herself caught in a fog—pulled into a picture she'd forgotten, lost and tumbled in all the gone years. Jinny stopped at her cabin door but didn't reach to open it, so arrested was she by the power of her memory. In her mind she could see the green boat, sailing away, and with it, Emma. Her red hair glinting in the sun off the water.

Jinny finally remembered that boat, that day, that beach. Jinny had stood and watched. She recalled crying, and then sitting in the sand, digging in the sand with her fingers. And there, beside her, was Deen. One head taller than she was. Deen saying, "Don't. Don't cry."

She remembered it with unusual clarity. His hair was tied back with a strand of dune grass, but not well. The strands kept slipping free. And he reached out and took her hand. For what must have been the first time. Took her hand, and led her away from the beach, up to the table. The two of them had ducked beneath it that day, just like Ess and Sam. Sat beneath the table, safe there, and Deen had pulled the dune grass from around his ponytail and held it out.

"For me?" she'd asked.

And he'd nodded as he reached down and tied it around her wrist. A gift.

That had been the beginning, hadn't it? Everything had been better after that. Everything Jinny could remember about anything had happened after that. How funny, to have forgotten something so important.

"Oh . . . ," whispered Jinny as she thought of Ess and Sam, giggling together. "Oh!" as if she'd stumbled onto something but only just barely recognized what it was.

A little while later they all stood, dressed and ready, around the fire circle. Ben passed out bags and baskets, and then they marched off in a line—up past the dunes and the cabins, along the sandy path, past the swink bushes, into the prairie and along the creek. Jinny couldn't remember the last time this had happened, the last time they'd all gone on a fetch together. She found herself happy, whistling. What was wrong with her lately? She needed to stop worrying so much.

Together they stopped to pick swinks. Together they hunted chicken eggs in the low branches of the trees and the tall grasses of the prairie, but when they came to the beehives, everyone but Jinny and Joon hung back. They were best with the bees, and there wasn't room for so many hands in the hives, lifting the dripping frames. Together the two oldest girls laid a clean sheet on the ground and got to work.

It was sunny in the glade. Good medicine, after the last few confusing days. Jinny inhaled the warm day and the smell of grass and dirt. She wondered idly if these bees were the same bees that had made honey for Abbie. Surely the hives must be the same. These were the children of the children of Abbie's bees, perhaps. It was a nice thought—Abbie lifting the lid, just this same way.

But when Jinny opened the box and reached in gently for the first frame of honeycomb, she found herself holding her breath. She wasn't sure why, but she suddenly felt a charge of energy, despite the lazy day and the sunny weather. As though the tensions of recent days had followed her up into the prairie and were buzzing along with the bees. Something stirred inside Jinny. She moved carefully, hesitantly. The bees felt somehow louder than usual. Not far away, Ess and Sam sat picking flowers beside a large boulder, while farther off, the others chased after what Jinny assumed to be a lizard or a kitten in the grass.

Just as Jinny was lifting the first panel free of the hive, and gently brushing the bees off it, she heard a shout and turned. Behind her she could make out Jak, Oz, and Loo racing toward her, arms in the air, streaking after a small black cat, who ran, ears back, tail low. Jinny stood, bees buzzing industriously around her head, honeycomb in hand, frozen, and watching.

She put up a hand to stop the boys barreling at her, to say *stop*. Only they didn't seem to notice. They kept coming, straight for her, chasing the cat. Jinny stared down at the bees covering the honeycomb in her hands, and she felt panic well up inside her. The bees were buzzing, and now Jinny was buzzing too. She took a breath and tried to calm herself. She braced for the hot sharp sting that would no doubt come when the shouting boys flew past. The calmer Jinny was, the less the stings would hurt. She knew this. And she knew stings weren't the end of the world. Like scratches and scrapes, they happened and healed.

Then, as if in slow motion, Jinny saw Ess rise from behind her boulder. The girl's face lit up. Ess grinned, called, "Kitty!" and tossed aside her handful of buttercups, which showered Sam, as Ess began to run. Now she careened toward Jinny too, in her lopsided gait.

Jinny was trapped, stuck. Her mouth opened to shout *Stop! No, stop!* but the bees buzzed and the air trembled with them. And as Jinny felt the hot bite of a single annoyed bee sting her hand, she had a flash, a vision of what would happen when clumsy Ess hit the hives. Ess, who couldn't ever seem to help knocking things over, whenever there were things to knock.

The bees had never done real harm before. But, Jinny thought, the morning pictures had never been blurry before. The nets had never been empty. And nobody had ever run smack into the hives. Jinny could do nothing but clutch the buzzing frame of dripping honey as she watched Ess careen her way.

Like she knew Ess would drool each night in her sleep, like she knew the stars would appear when the sun went down, Jinny knew what was going to happen next. She knew, and what could she do? She felt like she might choke.

"No, Ess, no!" shouted Jinny, shaking her head hard. She winced as her movement panicked the bees and she felt another sting. Sharp.

But it was too late. Ess bolted at Jinny, and in her rush of worry, Jinny did the only thing she could think of. She flung the frame of bees as far from her as she could, then ran forward, reaching out both arms, to catch Ess before the girl could hit the hive.

Unfortunately, as she did this, two other things happened. The cat changed direction, and the boys tore after it, doubled back toward the hives, straight into the path of the flying honeycomb. Before anyone else knew what was happening, the frame hit the ground near the boys and exploded, buzzing and transforming into an angry cloud of stingers. As one, the buzzing cloud seemed to constrict and condense, tighten into a knot of noise, a swarm of wings. And then, just as quickly, the knot unraveled as the bees dispersed, filled the air around Jak and Oz with speed and fire.

As screams filled the air, the cat became a scowling, snarling streak of dark fur. Jak and Oz fell to the ground, rolling and writhing. Loo, far behind them, stopped to stare. At the hive, Joon shouted a helpless "No!" And in the distance, the others began to race toward the disaster.

Clutching Ess, Jinny heard the shrieks and screams. She released the girl, turned, and ran to the boys. Ran *for* them. Everyone else was running too, but Jinny was closest.

"No, no, no, no, no!" she shouted, staring down at Oz and Jak.

Their eyes were closed, lips drawn tightly against gritted teeth as they rolled on the ground. Without thinking, Jinny dropped to her knees and began to beat at the boys with her bare hands, brushing and slapping the bees away as best she could, flinching at the stings on her hands. The others gathered around and stared at the trio, frozen, unsure of what to do.

In a matter of seconds, the bees flew off, but they left behind two boys covered in stings, angry red welts rising on their faces and arms. Tears in their eyes.

From the ground, Jak looked up and painfully opened one eye. "Jinny?" he whispered. "Are they gone?"

Jinny didn't know what to say. She looked down at the

tiny brown stingers stuck in her own burning hands. "I'm so sorry." She couldn't tell if the tears in her eyes were from the pain of her stings or something greater. Her chest was constricting. She could barely breathe.

"This is my fault. It's all my fault." She began to cry. "What did I do?"

That was when she felt someone push her out of the way, and Ben was there. Under his breath he said to her, "Calm down, Jinny. You're scaring everyone. The boys will be fine."

"But what if they aren't? What if . . ." Her voice faded.

"What are you talking about?" Ben hissed. "We've all had beestings before. It's okay."

"But that was . . . before!" she cried. This was different. Everything was different now. Didn't Ben feel the change?

Ben frowned. "Before *what*? Stop it, Jinny. You're overreacting. The littles are scared. Look!" He pointed up at Ess, Sam, and Loo, who all stared, wide-eyed, at Jinny.

"Before . . . ," she whispered, but then she looked at Ess's wide eyes and found she couldn't say more, or didn't want to.

Jinny peered down at her bee-stung hands. She tried to take a deep calming breath. But she couldn't help it. Instead, the breath shuddered inside her, and she burst into another storm of ragged tears.

"Jinny!" Ess snapped out of it and ran to her side, draping herself over Jinny. She reached for one of Jinny's hands with her own small fingers. But even for Ess, Jinny couldn't stop herself from crying.

"Hey, what's wrong, Jinny? Are you okay?" asked Oz, sitting up and wincing.

"Yeah, Jinny, you okay?" croaked Jak, as he pulled a stinger from his arm.

Ben still looked at her with a question in his eyes, but then shook his head. He stood up and clapped his hands, gave a whistle. "See? They're fine! All right, everyone! She's fine. We're all fine. Now come on. Let's get back home and clean ourselves up. Joon, can you finish the honey?" Without waiting for an answer, Ben marched away. "Come on—you too, Ess," he called. "Everyone, this way! Let's give Jinny a minute to herself."

Jinny sat alone, calmer, and yet still—not fine. She awkwardly wiped her face on her shoulder, sniffed back a runny nose, and stood up, her bee-stung hands stretched out in front of her. She managed to stop crying, but her face felt red and puffy, and she didn't trust herself to join the others. She wasn't ready to speak. She felt . . . fragile. Like she was built of broken bones.

Gingerly, Jinny stood up. She took her time, walked slowly, inhaling deep slow breaths as she made her way through the prairie. And thinking. Even as she calmed down, she knew that things were different now. These things that were happening that had never happened before . . . they weren't accidents.

And nobody could tell her different. Nobody would understand. Not Ben, not Joon. Not Ess.

"Would *you* believe me, Abbie?" she whispered as she walked. "I think you might."

When Jinny arrived back in the kitchen, the boys were sitting on a bench, joking and counting up their stingers, as Ben plucked them out with an old set of tweezers. They seemed to be in fine spirits. Jinny sat down on the other side of the table and sheepishly waited her turn. In the end, Jak won the bee-sting contest, with sixteen stingers extracted, including one on the tip of his nose. Oz had only eleven.

After Ben had applied slices of raw wild onion to their welts, he sent the boys off to rest. Then he came around the table and turned his attention to Jinny's hands. As he worked, she kept silent, but when he was done, she whispered, "Ben. I'm sorry." It felt like she was saying that a lot lately.

"It's fine," he said without meeting her eyes. It felt like he was saying *that* a lot lately.

"No, I . . . I shouldn't have done that, thrown the honeycomb that way. It was stupid, careless. I just . . . I saw Ess running at the hives, and I didn't think. I panicked."

"Don't be silly," said Ben, looking up. "Nobody blames you. It was quick thinking. Plus, the boys should know better than to run near the hives. Maybe *they* learned a lesson."

Jinny shook her head. "It shouldn't have happened."

Ben set down the tweezers and looked at Jinny thoughtfully,

as though he was deciding what to say. "You know what shouldn't have happened?" he said. "You getting upset like that around the littles. You scared them much worse than the bees did."

Jinny stared at her hands. "I know."

"Then why did you get so crazy, Jinny?"

Jinny shook her head. "I couldn't help it. I felt like it was my fault!" She felt her whisper turn into a sob. "My fault they got hurt."

"It happens, Jinny," said Ben. "People get hurt."

"But they shouldn't," said Jinny. "They never did before."

"That's not true," said Ben. "Remember when Joon fell out of the tree she was sleeping in that time and bent her finger back so far it didn't work for a while?"

"I guess," said Jinny.

Ben sighed and turned away from her. "I've never seen you like this before."

"I've never *felt* like this before. I don't know . . . how to talk about it."

"Well, I wish you'd at least try. We shouldn't keep secrets."

"No, we shouldn't," Jinny said.

Part of her wanted to talk to Ben, to open her mouth and let everything out, all the things she was afraid of, even if it didn't make sense. It would feel good to empty herself, she thought. But what would that do? If she truly explained her worries about the changing sky, the snake—if she told him that she feared she'd broken the island . . . that the sky might actually fall, like in the rhyme? That it felt, inside Jinny, like the sky was already falling? Then what? If Ben believed her, he might blame her, and if he didn't . . . She didn't know what was real, only her feelings, her fears, the things *inside* her. Nothing she could explain in a way anyone would understand.

"Anyway," said Ben, "we've spent enough time on this already, and I need to make dinner. Please go rest and get better, okay?"

"Okay," sniffed Jinny. She breathed deep, let it out in a rush. "I will."

But as she rose and made her way back to her cabin, she knew that wasn't a promise she could keep.

Jinny stared at the sky as she walked. The blue of it. Like an ocean above her, full of sun. It reminded her of her dream from that morning. It washed back over her, that warm bubble, that sense of closeness, of being held.

Jinny crossed her arms over her chest, gripped her shoulders in two white-knuckled hands. "Deen," she said. She closed her eyes and squeezed herself, hugged herself hard.

It didn't help anything.

21
Unfolding Wings

The next day at lunch, Eevie sat down and immediately wrinkled her nose. "Who *stinks?*" she asked, sniffing first Nat and then Sam on either side of her.

"That's not very nice, Eevie," cautioned Ben.

"No, it's not nice at all," said Eevie. "But neither is the smell. Like a rotten skunk pumpkin."

Jak and Oz burst out laughing.

"Not nice!" warned Ben. Then he sniffed the air himself, and he couldn't help wrinkling his own nose. "Skunk pumpkin? What's a skunk pumpkin?"

Eevie shrugged. "I don't know," she said. "Something stinky."

After that, everyone was sniffing the air and laughing

as they ate their lunch.

"Well," offered Joon, setting down her spoon, "I don't want to blame any one person, but truth be told, we could all use a bath. With everything that's been going on lately, we've gotten off our schedule, haven't we? Can anyone remember the last time we washed up?"

"It's been a while," Jinny admitted. "I guess that means it's washing-up day."

"Good idea," said Ben.

Joon stood and called down the table. "Hey! Everyone! Grab your things and meet at the fire circle as soon as you're done eating."

The kids all finished eating quickly and raced back to their cabins. Washing-up day on the island was a simple process, and everyone loved it. Each kid layered on all their clothes at once—their pants and tunic and sleeping shift too. Then they walked down the beach to the far side of the island, where the water was clear and there were no waves. There, in the sea-star field, they swam and played tag, until everything they owned was sopping wet and clean as they could get it. Their clothes, as they got wetter, became heavier, so it was a strange, slow game. After that, everyone walked back to dry in the hot sun. Nobody minded doing laundry.

When they arrived at the washing-up spot, Jinny was disappointed to realize she wouldn't really be able to join in, since Loo didn't know how to swim yet. Instead she sat at the water's edge, as she had done when Ess was littler, and watched the others jump and shout. She sighed as she rolled in the shallow water, cleaning herself as best she could and dreading Loo's swim lessons. Out in the water, she could see, Ess and Sam were swimming side by side, in some sort of game that involved spitting water into the air. She wondered what the game was. Then she remembered Loo beside her, and turned to discover that he was methodically tugging on one arm of a red sea star.

"Hey," she said. "Loo! What are you doing? Stop that!"

Loo looked up at her briefly. Jinny was sure he'd understood her, that her words had registered. But the boy simply blinked, then looked back down at the sea star and tugged again, harder.

"Hey, I mean it," Jinny said, more forcefully. "Cut that out!"

This time Loo didn't even look up. He just kept at it, torturing the soft body of the creature, pulling harder, stretching the tender thing as far as it would go. Jinny couldn't stand to watch, and she didn't like being ignored. She reached over with a quick hand, grabbed the sea star, and tossed it out into the water. Loo, surprised, opened his mouth and began to yell.

Listening to his screams, Jinny found herself sneering at the boy. It was like she was curdling inside, filling with anger. Stewing in it. What was *wrong* with this kid? As annoying as Eevie could be, she would never hurt a defenseless animal.

None of them would. How had Loo even thought to do such a thing? Where had that instinct come from?

"You know, Loo," Jinny said through gritted teeth, "it would sure be fun if you knew how to swim, wouldn't it?"

Loo looked puzzled. "Whah?" he said.

Jinny rose and leaned over Loo, towered above him in the shallows. "See," she said, "if you could swim, then you could play out there too. And I wouldn't have to sit here with you. Wouldn't you like to learn to swim?"

Loo looked up at Jinny. "No!" he shouted. "No, no, no!" He shook his head wildly back and forth.

"Oh, come on," she said. "You have to start somewhere. Like this." Jinny laid her long body down in the shallow water and showed him how to kick his feet and splash his arms at the same time, forcing a grin. "Now you try," she added.

"No!" shouted Loo.

Jinny reached up with one arm and tugged at Loo's leg, so that he lost his balance and toppled over beside her. He hit the surface with a splash, and Jinny was almost surprised by how good it felt, the motion of grabbing him, pulling him down, hearing the splash and his shout. Serves him right, she thought. Poor sea star.

But then . . . Loo sat right up, and with his eyes on Jinny the whole time, he reached into the water and pulled out another sea star. Right in front of Jinny's face, staring deep into her eyes, Loo began to tug. Again.

Jinny couldn't believe it. "Loo!" she shouted. She scrambled onto her knees beside him in the water. "Drop it!" she said. "I'm not kidding. Cut that out!"

Loo pulled harder than before, his expression unchanging.

"I *mean* it!" shouted Jinny.

With a quick, sharp tug, Loo yanked at the leg . . . and pulled it right off. "Ha!" he said, holding up the sea-star chunk proudly. He stuck out his tongue.

"*No!*" shouted Jinny. Before she knew what she was doing, her wet hand was slicing through the air swiftly. She felt Loo's small cheek explode against her palm. It stung like the bees, like a burn, full of prickles.

Loo gave a cry of pain and fell back over into the water. Jinny did too. They stared at each other, both of them shocked into silence, as the sea star and its leg fell from Loo's small hands.

Jinny stood up suddenly. "Ben!" she called, frantic. "Joon?"

Nobody came, and a fear rose inside Jinny, bubbling up in the back of her throat. What was happening to her? She had hit a Care. What *else* might she do?

"*Ben!*" she screamed. "Please, come, *now*!"

In a moment, Ben was by her side. "What is it? Are you okay? You need something?"

"Just . . . can you watch him?" asked Jinny. "Please? I need a minute. Just a minute. By myself."

Before Ben could answer, Jinny dashed forward into the water, dived under the surface, and swam out evenly in a straight line. Away. Away, away, away. Away from Loo, from the scene of what had just happened. She swam, to feel her own body pull and move. Jinny turned a somersault and felt the extra weight tugging at her skin, the odd heavyiness of her wet clothes. She wished she could take them off, strip this weight from herself. It was all so heavy, so terribly heavy.

She just needed to get away, away from everything, from all of them. Her whole world. Sometimes it was all too much, too close, too loud.

Jinny swam. And swam. And swam.

Walking home a little while later, her clothes baking in the sun, Jinny was silent. She trudged slowly, a little apart from the group. She couldn't help noticing that Ess was with Sam again, deep in conversation. Jinny wondered what they had to talk about so intently. It was good, she told herself, that they had finally found each other. So good. And yet . . .

When she passed the place in the cove where the boat sat up on the sand, beside the bell on its hook, Jinny stopped. The green paint was peeling in the sun. Jinny kicked the boat. "This is all your fault," she said. "Where did you come from? Why can't you tell me?"

Of course, the boat didn't reply. It just sat there. Jinny kicked it again, harder.

"Hey, now," said a voice behind her. "There's no need for kicking."

Jinny turned, flustered at being caught. "Oh, hi, Ben."

"Hey," said Ben. "Rough day?"

"Yeah, you could say that," said Jinny.

After a pause, Ben added, "Hey, Jinny . . . can I ask you a question?"

"Sure," she replied. "What is it?"

"Oh, just . . . do you think . . . ," Ben began, staring at where Jinny's foot had flaked off a bit of paint. "Do you think you'll ever go?"

Jinny stared at Ben. "I was just thinking about that. . . ."

"I wondered," added Ben. "Because maybe, one day, I might. Go. I mean, at some point, it would be time for me to go, right? Even if you don't? But I don't know when to go, with the boat on land like this. I don't know when it's my time."

"I hadn't . . . thought about that . . . very much," Jinny said slowly. It felt wrong, to be holding Ben back, and wrong not to tell him the things she knew. What if he had a mammaloo waiting for him, like Abbie? "Honestly, I hadn't thought about that at all."

"I can tell," said Ben.

Jinny turned. "What do you mean by that?" she asked.

"Nothing," said Ben. "Just that the rest of us are here too, you know?"

"Well, of course I do!" snapped Jinny.

"Sometimes it's hard to be certain what you know, or feel," said Ben with a shrug. "You don't . . . talk to me. Not the same way you used to. It makes it hard to tell you things."

Jinny squinted at the sun. How had they used to talk? She could hardly remember anymore. It occurred to her in that moment that if he wanted to, he could go, at any time. With no warning at all. Ben could just sail away, and she'd be left behind, without the boat, without any control at all. "You wouldn't . . . just go, without saying anything, would you? Take the boat and leave?"

Ben shrugged. "That doesn't sound like me, does it?"

"No," said Jinny. "It doesn't."

"But what difference would it really make if I did leave? I don't have a Care to worry about. It's one thing to feel like you're abandoning people, I guess. But I don't have anyone to abandon, do I? I don't have anyone who needs me."

"No. I don't guess you do," said Jinny.

Ben winced and, without another word, turned to walk away.

"Wait, no!" called Jinny. "We all need you, Ben."

But he kept on walking away.

Jinny let him leave. She watched him run on ahead. She waited. She didn't trust herself to walk beside him now. She might open her mouth. And the way she'd been feeling lately, she had absolutely no idea what could come out.

Everything was so wrong, so ruined. It was like the whole world was spoiled—the sky and everything beneath it. Jinny wished things could just go back. To the way they'd been *before*. Before Loo. *Loo*. Before things had begun to change. The island. And Jinny herself, on the inside. Before she'd ever felt like this, or imagined she could.

She hated this feeling. This sadness. Or . . . what was it? Not sadness exactly. Fury? Maybe both? She wasn't sure if she wanted to hit someone or cry. Only that there was a tightness in the back of her throat. A pull. A strain. Like there were words back there that wanted to fly out, like fire. Words she didn't know how to speak. Jinny thought it might help to scream, just scream, wordlessly. But then the others would all hear, and worry.

The others. Always the others. Always there, to think about.

Jinny looked down once more at the boat. The *boat*. The stupid boat. Jinny found herself clenching and unclenching her fists at the sight of it. Gritting her teeth.

Was this what Deen had felt, before the green boat arrived for him? Like he was suffocating?

And then Jinny wasn't angry at the boat. Suddenly it was as though she was staring at the cool blue sea on a broiling hot day. The boat was beautiful, a beautiful green. Soothing, even. Jinny longed for it, wanted to run to it, climb in. Suddenly, the boat looked like relief. All she had to do was drag it to the water and climb in. Then she could leave it all behind her. This feeling, and the island she loved.

But what kind of Elder would she be, to leave now? To leave her littles, just when their world was falling apart? No better than whoever had set her in a boat, releasing her to the sea. Only worse, because she'd broken the world she was abandoning them to. What kind of person broke the walls of the world, and then ran away as the roof fell in?

Oh, it would feel . . . free. She could imagine it. The cool wind cutting across the water on this hot day. She'd sit in the prow, close her eyes, leave it all behind her. And ahead of her would be . . . *what*?

A mammaloo of her own? Her . . . parents? If they existed? The ones who had set her in the boat to begin with? No, not them. They weren't real. Or if they were, they didn't matter. Which was pretty much the same thing.

But Deen. Waiting. Would he greet her? Would she tell him what she'd done? What had happened? All of it? What if she did? Would he understand? What would he say?

Nothing, he'd say nothing. Not at first, anyway. He was Deen. Jinny smiled as she imagined it. He'd fold her in big long arms. He'd rock her just a little, her head on his shoulder. He'd say, "Shh, it's okay." And then it would be. Because he'd be there.

Jinny closed her eyes. She tilted her face to the sun, shook her head slightly, and as her hair grazed her cheek, it was almost like Deen's hair, falling against her. And she wasn't so alone anymore.

Then the tears came. Rising, brimming. The green paint in front of her blurred. Jinny stood, rocking on her heels in the soft sand of the dunes, and shook her head hard, as all through her she felt a flutter. Like something was waking up inside her. A tiny bird in her belly, unfolding wings, and taking flight.

"Oh!" she gasped lightly, opening her eyes to the glaring sun. The boat in front of her was blurred by tears now, a smudge of green.

Jinny took off running, back to camp, back to the others.

22

From the Inside

Back at the cabin, Jinny found Loo and Ess curled up together, worn out and resting. She stared at them a second. They looked so sweet. What was wrong with her that Loo made her so crazy? And she seemed to bring out the worst in him too. What kind of Elder was she? She remembered that awful moment of the slap, the automatic rage inside her. Where had that part of her come from? What had woken it up?

"Hey, Loo, Ess," whispered Jinny. "How about I go and get some books for us to read? Shall we have a quiet story time?"

Loo eyed Jinny warily.

Ess registered his look, but she nodded. "Yes, please, Jinny."

So Jinny turned and left the cabin, trudged up the path. When she got to the book cabin, though, and was hunting through the books, Jinny found herself thinking not about Loo and Ess but about Abbie again. Each time she saw her name—Abigail Ellis—at the top of a book, or noticed her notes in the margins, she thought of the letter hidden back in her cabin.

It was such a funny thing, to feel as though she *knew* the long-gone girl. What, wondered Jinny, would Abbie have thought about Loo? What kind of an Elder had she been?

Jinny wished there was more of Abbie here for her, more clues tucked away. She wondered what the scribbled notes in all those buried books might have told her, if she'd ever had a chance to read them. She wondered if perhaps there were more letters hidden and waiting.

From her spot on the wrecked couch, Jinny found herself searching for another hiding place. Given that the first letter had waited all those years to be found, it seemed at least possible that there might be more of them. The books had all been flipped through a thousand times by one kid or another, but what about other nooks and crannies in the room? Jinny stood up, and then slowly she walked, running her hand along the undersides of windowsills, staring up at the ceiling, trying to imagine that there was some corner of the room she'd never considered. She walked every inch of the little cabin, touching all the floorboards with her toes, feeling for a loose panel. But in the end, there was nothing.

At last she lay down on the floor, annoyed, and stared at the mildewed ceiling. But when she did, something caught her eye—a glimpse of something pale, something white, glowing in the dark recesses under the couch. Something wedged up inside the springs. Jinny scooched over and turned on her side to wriggle and stretch a long arm under the sofa. Then she reached up, tugged, felt the tips of her fingers graze a slip of paper. Her heart raced. She repositioned herself, craned her neck, twisted her body, and managed to reach in a little farther and snatch at it. Something tore, gave way, and when she withdrew her hand, she found she was indeed holding a piece of paper.

"'Do not remove tag from sofa,'" Jinny read aloud. She groaned and let the scrap of paper fall from her hand as she struggled to her feet. But when she leaned over to grab her stack of books from the table, Jinny froze. There was a smear of blood on her calf. She couldn't begin to imagine where it had come from. Had she scraped herself, wriggling under the couch? But, no, there were no scratches on her legs at all. As she wiped the blood off with her hand, she backtracked in her mind and couldn't think of anyplace. She was as clean as a person could be, her hair still slightly damp from the water in the sea-star field, while her clothes had dried in the sun.

When Jinny stood up, she noticed more blood, a stain on her tunic, where it must have been bunched up while she was sitting. She glanced over her shoulder, to be sure the door was shut, and then she leaned down and examined her pants. Sure enough, there was a little more blood, seeping through the thin fabric between her legs. Had she cut herself *there*? How?

Praying nobody would burst in on her, Jinny loosened her drawstring and then reached a hand down inside the pants to pat between her thighs. When she withdrew her fingers, they shouted with blood, bright and red. The sight made Jinny's stomach turn over. She was bleeding *there*. She was bleeding from the *inside*. Was she broken? Had she cracked, somehow, inside herself? And how could she fix it? Would all her blood seep out?

What did this mean? She had no idea and nobody to ask. She looked around the book cabin and tried to think of a story where something like this happened. People in books got killed by bullets, arrows, and wild dragons. They bled all the time, but not like this. She'd never read about anything like this. What was wrong with her? "Oh, Abbie," she called out to the silent room. "What do I do?" But of course there was no answer.

Suddenly, she recalled a moment. Deen, by the boat. "The world might break to bits," he'd said. It was just some words, a story he'd made up. But now the mist was thinning, and here she was, breaking. Breaking to bits. Was it possible they were all connected—one to another? The sky, her body. The hissing snakes and the angry bees, the empty nets, and Loo. All broken, part of the same disaster. It was her fault. And she was the only one who knew it, that the world was unraveling.

Jinny jumped to her feet before she could make a bigger mess and ran next door to the store cabin, where she pulled off her stained pants and tunic. Then she wiped herself roughly between the legs over and over, as though she might somehow stop the bleeding that way. She pulled a torn sleeping shift from the ragbag and, using her teeth to start, she ripped it into several strips. She tied them together, so that she had a thin piece of fabric, several yards long. Then Jinny bound herself. She started by wrapping the cloth around her waist, like a belt. She knotted it, and then passed the fabric between her legs, where the blood was. Over and over she did this, until it felt thick and bulky, uncomfortable, and tight. But secure. She wrapped herself, until that part of her, the bleeding part, was covered with a good thick inch of cloth. As though she could bind herself back together with rags, keep her body from coming apart at the seams, keep her bits from breaking. Finally, she slipped into a fresh tunic and pants and darted to the wishing cabin, where she dropped the bloody clothes into the wishing hole.

Satisfied that she was covered up, and that nobody had seen anything, Jinny dashed down to the kitchen to wash her hands from the scalding kettle of water on the cookstove. She splashed her hands with the dipper and winced, but somehow the pain felt right, good.

So. Now she knew for certain. Her body had shown her. Deen had been right and Jinny had been wrong, and everything she did only made things worse.

If she left, if she climbed into the green boat now, was there any chance the mist might knit itself magically back together? Would the pictures return to the sunrise sky? Would she, Jinny, heal on the inside? Or would she just be running away if she left now, deserting the others, stranding them on the island she'd broken? That seemed very wrong. Escaping to that other place, wherever it was, and leaving everyone else behind in a fracturing world. She couldn't do that. Most of all, she couldn't bear the thought of leaving Ess to an island she'd broken. She'd thought she was holding on to her life, when really she'd been strangling it, gripping it so tightly it shattered.

And if she did leave now, if she could bring herself to do that, what would she find out there, beyond the mist? How could she know it would be any better? How could she be sure of anything?

Jinny looked around her as she walked back to the sleeping cabin, and it brought tears to her eyes to see how normal everything seemed. The dishes gleaming on the drying rack, and Eevie and Nat sitting at the end of the dock. They didn't know. Only Jinny knew what was happening. And yet the knowing didn't make her feel stronger or smarter. She'd never felt so unsure before, so lost. It was exactly the same feeling she'd had in the sea, when she'd realized she could no longer see the island. Helpless. Adrift.

Back in the cabin, Loo had fallen asleep. But Ess was sitting up in the bed, eyes wide open, waiting for Jinny.

"What book?" whispered Ess, as Jinny perched beside her on the bed.

Jinny groaned. "Oh, I'm sorry, Ess. I totally forgot to bring the books. I got distracted."

"Why?" asked Ess.

Jinny paused, not knowing how to answer. "Because I had to fix something, in the storeroom," she said at last.

"Why?"

"Because it was broken."

"Why?" asked Ess again, tilting her head to one side and staring at Jinny.

Jinny suddenly had the odd feeling that Ess wasn't actually asking her a question so much as she was daring her to answer.

"I don't know," said Jinny, sitting down on the edge of the bed. Tears sprang into her eyes and she moved to wipe them away, but not before Ess had noticed. The little girl got onto her knees and crawled over to Jinny. She sat down beside her and put a thin arm over the bigger girl's shoulder. "It'll be okay, Jinny. Right?"

"I hope so, Ess," said Jinny, closing her eyes. "I really do."

Ess gently laid something in her lap, and Jinny opened her eyes again. It was the grubby bracelet made of shoestrings. "What's this for, Ess?" she asked, holding it up.

"For you," said Ess, smiling. She patted Jinny on the hand. "Mama is for you now. To fix it. Make you happy."

Despite everything—her cramping belly, the tightness of her bindings, and the heavy knowledge she carried inside her—Jinny did smile then. She couldn't help it. No matter what, some things were still good and whole and true.

23

Unbreaking the World

When Jinny woke up each morning after that, it was with a strange dark feeling. As though something was pulling at her, tugging at her hem. A warning. The two children sleeping peacefully in the bed above her gave no particular cause for alarm, and yet, as Jinny piled her cushions and slipped into her clothes every day, she couldn't shake her worry. It grew.

All Jinny wanted was for the world to feel the way it had before the boat arrived with Loo. And so she fished and fetched. She helped Ben in the kitchen, and smiled even when she didn't feel like smiling. She'd never been so diligent before, so focused. She didn't argue with Eevie. She didn't say anything when Ess disappeared with Sam to play, leaving her behind. Please, please, please, she thought. Let it be okay. If she could only keep the changes at bay. If she could only keep things the way they were.

But no matter how many crabs she caught, no matter how many plomms she pitted, the sky each morning was hazy and bleary. The pictures were gone. The haul from the nets was smaller and smaller. And Jinny carried the dragging feeling with her.

At least when Jinny unwound her rags one morning, she found her bleeding had stopped. She stared at the dark-brown stains and wondered if, maybe, things could go back to the way they had been before. Maybe she'd learned her lesson, and the island knew it and forgave her? If only there was some way to know. If only there was a way to check, to test the island, to see that it was healing. Jinny decided to take a long walk. Perhaps the bees would be calm after all, the snakes silent, and the chickens full of eggs.

"I'm going on a fetch," she said to Ben, when she found him in the kitchen. "So if there's anything you need, let me know. I think I'll walk along the beach to the sea-star fields, and then cut across the prairie and head up the cliffs. That way I can get the last batch of dried snaps, and we can make honeyed snaps for a treat. How does that sound?"

"Wow, that's a long walk," said Ben. "Any particular reason?"

Jinny shrugged. "I just feel like walking," she said.

"Are you going to take the littles with you, or should I watch them here? That might be too much for them. Don't you think?"

"If you don't mind," Jinny said, "I'd love to go by myself. You sure that's okay?"

Ben nodded, and Jinny ran back to tell Ess, with a snap bag over her shoulder, whistling. But it wasn't so simple.

"I want to come too," Ess said firmly.

Jinny sighed. "No. This one time, I want to go alone. Just me."

"Why?" demanded Ess.

Jinny didn't know how to explain the *why* of it. "Because . . . sometimes, it's nice to be alone."

Ess looked worried. "It's nice to leave me behind?"

"Not you, Ess. Just . . . nice to have a little quiet."

Suddenly there were tears in Ess's eyes. "You're leaving. You're going away, like Oz and Jak said."

"No!" cried Jinny. "Oh, Ess, no, no, I'm not. I just . . . I'm tired, and want to take a walk alone."

"Promise?"

"I promise."

Ess still looked so sad. "Promise you'll never, ever, ever leave?"

Something twisted inside Jinny, at the question and the sight of the sad girl. But "I promise" somehow slipped from her lips. Consoled, Ess ran off to find Sam.

After the discomfort of that conversation it felt extra good to be able to move fast, to walk hard, *away*. As she made her way down the path, past the cabins, and then along the beach in the direction of the bone tree, Jinny stopped to look back at her island. She could see Oz and Jak hunting for something in the dunes. Probably crabs or scuttles. She spotted Nat reading a book. Ess and Sam were back under the table, playing some sort of game. Everything seemed so calm, so normal. Maybe that was true. Maybe everything was fine again. Jinny would see for herself.

She took a deep breath, smiled, and tried to enjoy her walk. She stared into the tide pools, where everything looked as it always had. The petalfish glowed purple and green. She walked along the sea-star field and gazed out at the flat calm water. Then she headed up into the prairie. She opened the hives and peered in, to find happily buzzing bees, busy at their constant work. Every step she took, Jinny felt a little bit better.

Farther up the prairie, a kitten tore past Jinny's feet, in play. And a few minutes later, she marched through a cluster of chickens hunting bugs in the grass. Everything was fine. Everything was utterly usual. The sun was shining, and a breeze was blowing, and Jinny could find nothing to worry about. So why did she still feel . . . nervous? All the time, every moment. Even with the birds singing above her as she climbed up to the cliffs. It was all a little too perfect.

By the time she arrived at the flat rocks above, Jinny noticed clouds were roiling out over the water. And it was almost a little satisfying, the imperfection, the threat of rain. I'll work fast, she thought to herself. I'll work double fast.

Jinny ran to and fro, as quickly as she could, picking up the sweet dark snaps, sticky with crystallized sugar. Now and then she popped one into her mouth, bit through the tight, thick outer skin to the sweet gummy fruit that stuck wonderfully to her teeth, and spat out the slick pit onto the stone. *Thhpt.*

Jinny was almost finished when she turned and remembered something. She and Deen had another game they'd played with the wind. Deen would stand below, on the rock cliff, and Jinny would step very intentionally, out into a gust of wind, holding his hands, to keep her from falling right back. There, sometimes, she'd fly. When the wind was right, and Deen's grasp was firm, Jinny could stay like that for long moments. Up in the air, the wind in her face, breathless.

"Don't *you* want to fly?" Jinny would ask him, when she was done.

Deen would shake his head, and flash her a quick bright grin. "No, I like to watch you," he'd say. "Plus, I'm too big. You couldn't hold me down, I don't think. Just imagine how bad you'd feel if I flew away."

"You goof," Jinny'd tell him. "The island wouldn't let that happen."

But by then they'd be on their way back down. Sliding, shouting.

Now, standing alone with her memory, Jinny realized that "flying" wasn't a game she'd play with anyone else. Deen had been right. It would feel funny to trust someone smaller than herself to hold her down. With Deen gone, there was nobody left to be her ballast. Jinny hefted her bag up over her shoulder, and then she noticed something—that the rushing, roaring wind that usually swirled around the cliffs wasn't as loud as usual.

That was strange. Jinny stopped for a moment, pondering how to check it. At last she opened one of her bags, pulled out a handful of fruit, and tossed the sweets gently over the edge. But rather than flying back at her, bouncing against the wall of wind, the fruits fell, plummeted over the edge to the waves below. Jinny walked closer and leaned over. She stared down, down into the water, and felt a tremble, a strange sense that she was in terrible danger. As though her feet might suddenly decide to leap off the cliff without asking her head for advice.

Jinny lowered herself shakily, placed her hands flat on the warm rock beneath her, and closed her eyes. She tried to steady herself, and to hold down her breakfast. She sat a moment, thinking. Attempting to think. Well, it can't get worse now, she thought. This is the worst thing I can imagine. But in fact, that wasn't true. Jinny could imagine far worse. Of course she could.

At last she forced herself to stand, hefted the straps of the bag up on one shoulder again, and made her way across the flat stone surface, to where she could slide easily back down to the prairie. But for the first time ever the ride didn't feel like pleasure. It was only speed, a necessity. Jinny wanted to be home *now*. Wanting to get away, she had come out today, walking. She'd pretended she was hunting for signs of safety, but that had been make-believe, a dream. Really, she'd been looking for danger, and she'd found it. Underneath her thrumming fear, there was some twisted satisfaction in having found what she was searching for.

As stray drops began to pelt her head, she tore through the prairie, ahead of the rain, not stopping to look out for the kittens. Not stopping to pick flowers at the stream. Jinny dashed back into camp, breathless, and collapsed near the fire circle.

"Here," she said, panting. "Snaps. And there's heavy rain coming, I think."

"Thanks," said Ben. "Glad to have them. But are you okay? You seem awfully rushed. Why so worried about a little rain?"

Jinny leaned against the table and tried to catch her breath. "It's not that. It's . . . much worse." She panted. "Something is bad, wrong."

Ben regarded Jinny in that delicate way that she was starting to hate. "Day rain isn't anything to get so alarmed about."

"Ben!" she cried. "Just stop! Stop it!" The shout flew from Jinny, took her by surprise. It shocked Ben too. He looked unsettled.

"It's *not* okay," said Jinny. "Do you understand me? Stop trying to make things fine. Things are not fine!"

"What do you mean? *What's* not fine?"

Jinny wanted to shake Ben, hard. He was so frustrating! And so blind. *Everything*, she wanted to say. *Absolutely everything*. She wanted to tell him about the blood on her legs and the dreams she'd been having. She wanted to shout that the very air felt wrong, even when the weather was perfect. She wanted to show him the fin that had risen above her head, and Loo's face when she'd struck it. She wanted him to know that she was always waiting, waiting, waiting . . . for something terrible to happen. But he wouldn't understand any of that. He wasn't ready, and he didn't want to. So instead she took a deep breath and said, "The wind."

"The wind?"

"The wind! The wind has died down, up at the cliffs. I threw some snaps over the edge, and the wind didn't catch them. They fell."

"Fell where?" asked Ben.

"All the way. Down. To the water."

"Ohhhh," said Ben slowly. "Oh. Well, *that's* no good." He looked thoughtful, like he was taking in what she'd just told him, turning it over in his mind. "If that's true, we need to be sure the littles don't go up there without us, ever. Or until things fix themselves."

"Yes," said Jinny. "In fact, maybe *nobody* should go up there. Ever. It didn't feel . . . safe. Not even for me."

"I wonder what's going on," said Ben, eyeing her carefully. "First the sky changed, and the mist seems thinner. Now this."

"See!" shouted Jinny. "See! I'm *not* crazy. I'm not imagining it all. Something *has* changed." She looked at Ben's even gaze, knowing what he was finally realizing. That this was her fault. She wished he'd just say it, get it over with.

"Well," said Ben. "It's good to know, but we can't do much about it right now, can we? So let's get to work on these candies. The kids will be excited." He turned around, busied himself in the kitchen. "Why don't you chop the nuts?"

Jinny paused for a moment, waiting to see if that was really all he was going to say. How could he not make the connection, blame her? She would blame someone if she could, that was for sure. But Ben didn't. He wasn't a blaming person. Ben was nice. He wasn't going to get upset, and he wasn't going to scold Jinny, and he wasn't going to notice that the world was ending. He was just going to make some nice candies for the kids.

It made Jinny want to scream. But she didn't. She got to work on the nuts.

24
Snake in the Grass

The next day, after a thin lunch of crabs and sorrel salad, Jinny shared the platter of candies. "Hey, look, everyone. Sweets!" Though her own excitement felt false, it cheered her some to hear the cries of surprise and pleasure, and to feel the grubby, grabbing hands reaching toward her. At the other end of the table, Ben smiled warmly.

But Ess's eyes widened as Jinny came to her with the candies. "Where's mama?" she asked.

"Huh?" said Jinny, setting down the platter.

"Mama?" Ess pointed at Jinny's bare wrist.

"Oh," said Jinny. "I . . . I don't know. It must have fallen off, back in our cabin. Why don't we finish lunch, and then I'll go put mama back on. Okay?"

"Okay," said Ess. But her eyes barely left Jinny's wrist during the meal. And Jinny's hopes that the girl might forget the bracelet altogether faded when Ess swallowed her last bite and immediately hopped down from her spot on the bench. She said, "Now we'll find mama."

"Sure," said Jinny. "Of course we'll look." She followed Ess up the path.

Mama was not in the sleeping cabin, in the bed, or under it. She wasn't in the book or wishing cabin. As the search continued, Ess's eyes seemd to grow in her face, and her mouth tightened into a thin horizontal line. She didn't speak a word, and Jinny wondered the whole time about all the things the girl wasn't saying. It wasn't like Ess to be so quiet. As the two of them walked up and down the beach in painful silence, Ess periodically stopped to root in the sand with a dirty foot, but it did no good. There was no sign of mama.

When they returned to the kitchen, Ben asked, "No luck?"

Ess only shook her head, her face still masklike. The sight broke Jinny's heart.

"Did you maybe lose it up at the cliffs yesterday?" asked Eevie, who was standing at the table scraping the honey from the candy platter with a finger. "Have you looked there?"

Ess looked up and broke her silence. "The cliffs?"

"Thanks, Eevie," said Jinny through gritted teeth. "That's a *big* help."

"Let's go!" Ess shouted.

"You know," offered Ben, "it's been drizzly on and off the last few days. Maybe it would be better to wait until tomorrow. When it's sunny. You don't want to get stuck up at the cliffs in the rain, do you? It'll be slippery. Maybe you should wait."

Ess shook her head. "No. What if it rains, and mama is lost in the mud?"

"No, Ben's right. That's a good idea," agreed Jinny. "Let's wait until tomorrow. Don't you agree, Eevie? Don't you think it's a good idea?"

Eevie shrugged. "Sure. I guess."

Jinny wanted to strangle her, but she turned to smile at Ess as convincingly as she could. "Ess, let's wait a day. In the morning it'll be sunny and fine, and I'll go up there and find mama for sure. I promise, okay?"

"No," Ess said, and shook her head. "Now, today."

"Come on." Ben tried to help. "Mama isn't going to go anywhere. If it's there now, it'll be there later. Right?"

"No!" Ess shouted suddenly. "No, no, no!"

Like an echo, Loo shouted too. "No, no, no!" Jinny wasn't sure he even understood what was happening. He just liked to yell.

Everyone looked at Jinny, to see what she'd do. Ess had never, in all those sleeps, behaved quite like this. "Ess," Jinny begged, "please, understand—it's not a safe day for the cliffs."

"Mama!" Ess cried, and burst into tears. "I want mama and you don't care about mama, and I gave mama to you and you lost her and everything is bad now."

Jinny tried to go to her, to hold her. But Ess pushed her away and pummeled Jinny's chest with her bony arms.

"Ow! Look, Ess," Jinny snapped, holding the girl at arm's length. "You can't just do whatever you feel like whenever you want to. You can't hit me, and you can't tell me what to do. I'm the Elder, and you're my Care. Do you understand me?"

Ess looked up at Jinny, suddenly motionless and silent. She didn't nod. But she stared Jinny in the eyes, her mouth lightly open, as if there was something she wanted to say but wouldn't.

Jinny continued, in the new firm voice she'd somehow found inside herself. "It's going to rain again soon, and it's late in the day already. It doesn't make any sense to go now. I'll take you tomorrow, and that's going to have to be good enough. Got it?"

Ess's mouth snapped shut. She stared at Jinny. "I got it," she said softly. Then she turned and began to walk away, head down, toward the path past the kitchen.

"Hey. Wait, where are you going?" Jinny called after her in a gentler voice.

"I hafta go wish," Ess called over her shoulder. "Okay? Am I allowed to wish?"

"Sure," said Jinny, staring after her. "Of course you are. And I'll walk down the beach a little ways, look for mama some more there. Okay?"

Ess nodded silently, her back still turned, as she headed up the path, alone.

Jinny spent the next hour combing the beach, with Loo running ahead on the dunes. She knew mama wasn't there. She didn't think she'd even walked down the beach this direction since Ess had given the bracelet to her, but she wanted to walk, to stretch and think. She only wished Loo had stayed behind. She couldn't think with him there—he was too distracting, with his constant yells and bellows.

When she got back, she handed Loo off to Ben, who was chopping something green in the kitchen, and then headed for her cabin. It would be nice, after the rough afternoon, to spend a little time with Ess, alone. Ess deserved it, and Jinny could use a hug herself. She needed to feel like things were okay again. She would close her eyes and bury her face in Ess's hair, and everything would feel better.

But Ess wasn't in their cabin. She wasn't in the book cabin either. Jinny stood on the ridge and shouted for her. "Ess?" There was no answer, so she ran down the path to the beach. Then she doubled back to the kitchen, shouting, "Ben. Joon. Tell me you've seen Ess? Please!"

Jinny only meant to take Joon. Joon, who ran faster and climbed better than anyone else. But nobody wanted to stay behind when they realized Ess was missing, so somehow Jinny found herself at the head of a herd. They trampled together up the path above the cabins, heading for the prairie. Ben carried Loo on his shoulders. They called Ess's name as they marched. All their voices, high and low, soft and loud, mingling together. *Ess!* Rain began to fall, faint but cold, and nobody said a word, not even Eevie.

Jinny prayed the whole way up the sandy path, past the cabins, and along the stream: Not the cliffs, not the cliffs, not the cliffs. We need to find her before the cliffs. But she knew. Deep in her gut, she knew. Over and over she remembered her handful of snaps, falling through the wind, hurtling down the sheer rock face into the churning, bashing water far below.

And she remembered another day too—Ess joyfully tossing her thin body up into the billowing breeze, laughing into the sunlight, and trusting it. She remembered her words to the little girl: "The cliffs won't let you fall," she had said. Jinny's stomach roiled as she put these memories together. She ran faster and panted. Not. The. Cliffs.

Ess wasn't near the swink bushes, or taking cover from the rain in the trees where the hens liked to sleep. She wasn't making clover chains. But when Jinny stepped out of the high grasses of the prairie, into the hilly mounds of boulders at the base of the cliffs, she looked up into the sky and saw a shape moving against the rock.

Jinny shouted. "There!"

Everyone stopped to follow her gaze, and together they all

found a black head of hair bobbing above them, above the sea of grass, climbing the boulders, halfway up and moving fast.

"Ess!" Jinny shouted, as her voice broke with relief, and she began to run again. "Ess!"

Ess heard the voice in the wind, whipped her head around, and saw Jinny, but she didn't wave or respond, only kept on climbing. Jinny sprinted toward her, the others following, until they were all standing at the base of the boulders, peering up at Ess, a shape against the stone.

"I'm going to throttle that girl," shouted Eevie. "I'm soaking wet already."

"Shut up, Eevie," said Ben. Jinny turned to him in surprise. She had never heard words like that come from his mouth. Eevie looked stunned too. Ben shrugged and, in a gentler voice, added, "There's a time and place for everything."

"Why don't we just give her a minute?" offered Nat sensibly. "She's sure to get tired and come down, isn't she?"

But Jinny couldn't wait. She couldn't do nothing. The rocks would be slick in the rain, and Ess was so clumsy. She pulled herself up onto the first boulder and shouted, "Please, come back here, Ess!"

When Ess saw Jinny climbing up behind her, she shot the older girl an angry look, turned back around, began to climb faster.

"I bet she's afraid she's in trouble," said Oz.

"Is she in trouble?" asked Jak.

"She should be," grumbled Eevie, with a careful glance at Ben.

Beside her, Loo let out a catlike growl. "Tubble!" he shouted.

"No, she's not in trouble, and she's not afraid," said Jinny sadly. "She's mad. At me."

With her hands on the dirty wet boulders just above her head, Jinny squinted into the cloudy sky. She was itching to climb, but when she hoisted herself up onto the next rock, she felt it shift slightly under her weight. The boulders had always been sturdy, before. But Jinny wasn't sure what might happen anymore. Even on a good day, without rain, Ess tended to topple. So Jinny forced herself to stand still and called out, "Ess! Come down, please!" Her voice cracked, and she had to work to keep from crying.

As Ess scrambled up the next boulder, Jinny began to shake. If Ess slipped and fell, Jinny was sure she could snap a bone or crack her skull. Or worse. What was worse?

Jinny longed to do something. She needed to grab hold of Ess, needed to stroke her tangled hair, clutch her thin shoulder. "I said come down here, and I mean it!" she screamed up at Ess. But the girl kept climbing.

A few minutes later, Ess ran out of boulders. When she reached the very top, she pivoted, slowly reaching her arms out for balance. "Mama . . . isn't . . . here . . . ," she cried. She sounded angry, but at least she was talking now.

"Come down, Ess!" shouted Jinny. She tried to sound warm. "I'm not mad anymore. Don't you be mad either. Please come down."

"When I find mama!"

"She isn't there," said Jinny. "I didn't go up that way." She added, "Please."

Ess looked down at Jinny. She didn't reply.

"I'll find mama for you," called Jinny, "I swear. Just come here."

Ess stared down at Jinny, and Jinny waited, miserable, until another voice behind her called out, "Ess! Ess, please come back!" Jinny had never heard Sam yell in his life. He wasn't sniffling, and he wasn't quiet. "You need to come down!" he shouted. "Please? I miss you!"

As Jinny watched, Ess seemed to consider. She tilted her head and peered down the boulders at the boy.

"Yes!" called Jinny. "Yes, come down for Sam, Ess!" she cried. "Sam is worried."

"Don't be worried, Sam!" shouted Ess. "I'm okay. See?" Then she turned and began to lower herself down the boulder she'd just climbed, sliding on her belly.

Jinny took a deep shuddering breath. Relief.

But a moment later, Ess shouted. "Oh, no! I can't, Jinny!" Still clinging to the top boulder, she was too short to touch the rock below with her toes.

"You can do it," said Jinny. "Just drop. It's only a few inches."

From below, Loo piped up. "Loo climb too!"

Jinny ignored him.

Then Eevie shouted, "You got up there yourself. Now get yourself down."

"Shut *up*, Eevie!" chorused several voices.

"Jinny?" cried Ess, still hanging from her boulder. "My hands are tired." Her voice shook. "I'm scared now."

"It's okay," said Jinny, beginning to climb in earnest now. "I'm coming."

Below her, the others waited, but they didn't matter now. Not to Jinny. The sunrise shapes and the winds didn't matter either. Only Ess. Only this moment. All Jinny could hear was Ess, calling for her. All she could see was the shape of her girl, suspended in the rain and against the rock. "I'm coming, Ess," she called out. "Hang on. You're doing great."

"Okay, Jinny!" Ess called out. "Okay, I'm hanging!" She began to cry.

"Ess," called Jinny weakly as she climbed, "just wait there. Don't move."

Ess waited, and Jinny began to climb surely and quickly. After the first few boulders, she turned to look down and saw the others below, their eyes trained on her. All but Loo, who'd wandered off a ways, to hunt something in the high grass nearby. Jinny watched him jump in the grass a moment, then turned and reached for the next bit of rock above her head. She didn't have time for Loo right now, or anyone below. She couldn't care about anything else—just the boulders beneath her shaking fingers, the girl stranded on them, and her own tired body. Only one direction mattered—up.

At last Jinny reached the top, reached Ess. She raised her hands to grip Ess around the waist, and felt the girl fall limply into her grasp. Then Jinny lowered herself to sitting, to rest, with Ess in her lap, and felt a warm rush of calm all through her. She loved the sturdy boulder beneath her dearly. She loved the cold rain. She loved holding Ess, and sitting a moment. She loved everything. "You're okay," she said. "Even without mama. Okay?"

"Okay," Ess said, nodding, her face streaked with dirt and tears. She leaned back into Jinny.

"And you will never run away like that again, will you?"

Ess shook her head. "I don't think so."

Jinny smiled at that, gave the girl a squeeze, and then looked down and waved to the faces far below her. "We're coming down!" she shouted. "Everything is fine! Everything is—"

And then she realized something—that in the huddle of kids below, Loo was nowhere to be seen. Jinny cast her glance in every direction and couldn't find him. She'd seen him only a moment before, hadn't she?

"Hey, Ben," she shouted down. "Can you see—"

Then.

A scream.

An earsplitting scream. A piercing cry from somewhere close, in the grass. Terror. Loo only screamed once, high and long and loud.

Jinny frantically scanned the ground below her, but in the rain and the dull cloudy light, she couldn't find the boy anywhere in sight. She could only hear his fear ringing in the air. The others were bustling now, hunting for him, but *she* was his Elder. He was her Care.

"Ess?" said Jinny, lifting the girl from her lap, and rising. "We need to—"

"Go!" said Ess, looking shocked and wet and cold. "Go to Loo, Jinny! Go!" With a quick nod, Jinny turned and dived—half running, half tumbling down the boulders.

By the time Jinny reached Loo, the others had formed a circle around him. But nobody was moving. Nobody was touching him. Everyone was frozen. Afraid. Silent. The only thing that made a sound was the rain.

Loo sat on the ground in the high grass, legs spread wide. In between them, the snake stretched up, vertical, as though it had sprouted there, grown as a seed from the earth and now impossibly tall. Its mouth was open in a tense yawn. Its teeth were needles. And it made a strange rattling sound Jinny had never heard before. Like a warning, or an end.

Loo was motionless. His face gone white. His eyes closed.

Nobody moved. It was as though they'd all been painted into a picture. Drawn on a flat white stone. The moment lasted forever.

Or it took no time at all. A flicker, a second. It was hard to know. The snake stared, its tongue a thin, quick flame. Its taut silence had spread to all of them. Nobody spoke. Loo was a statue. Jinny wondered how long this could last. And what could she do? What should she *not* do?

Then Loo couldn't take it anymore. He opened his eyes, stared into the snake's mouth, and screamed at the top of his lungs, "YAAAAAAAAAH!"

The snake was a whipcrack. Its head jerked sharp, the teeth sank, Loo shrieked again and shook his leg violently, so that the snake flew off, like a rope tossed into the grass.

Quickly, Jinny fell to the ground and reached for him. "Loo? Loo? Are you okay?" But of course he wasn't. Jinny knew from books what snakes could do, what the poison in their fangs could do. Tears were rolling down his face. "Ow-ow-ow-ow," he cried, sounding younger than he ever had before.

"Ben," Jinny called as she heaved the boy up into her arms, "I've got him. You run ahead and find a book, if there's a book. What do we do?" Loo's foot was swelling already. She began to run, as fast as she could, struggling with the child in her arms and the high grass.

Jinny ran, through the prairie and down the path, over

the ridge, and home. It took forever. It took no time at all. It was all a rush of fear and guilt and the shuddering child in her arms. By the time Jinny reached the cabin, Loo wasn't moving anymore. His eyes had rolled shut and his foot was twice its normal size. Was there anything she could do? she wondered. How long did they have?

Ben dashed into the room. "There's a book! The first-aid book. It says to tie a band between the bite and his chest. So the poison can't get to his heart."

Jinny looked wildly around the room. A band? She pulled the drawstring from her pants, kicked them off, and reached down to tie the string as tightly as she could above Loo's foot, around the fat strong child leg, the thick calf muscle. She turned back to Ben. "Now what? What else?"

Ben shook his head. "I'm sorry. That's it. That's all there is. It just says to do that, with the band, and then to keep him as still as possible. Not to move him. Depending on the type of snake, he might need something called antivenin, medicine we don't have. There are words I've never seen before. Not sure how to pronounce them, even."

"What?" Jinny shouted, too loudly. Everyone looked up, startled. Jinny was hot with anger, quick with rage. It made no sense. "Why would anyone send us to a place with snakes and not give us snake medicines, if there *are* such things? What kind of parents do we have that they shipped us off to a place like this?"

"We don't," said Ben quietly, shaking his head. "We don't have parents. Why would you even say that?"

"Never mind," said Jinny quickly. "Just . . . *why are we here*?"

"I don't know. . . ." Ben sounded scared now. Jinny couldn't remember him ever sounding that way. Ben was supposed to be the *fine* one. She counted on him being fine.

"We're supposed to be safe here! Aren't we supposed to be safe?"

"I don't know anymore," he said again, quieter this time.

"So now what do we do?" asked Jinny.

"We wait, I guess," said Ben. "And hope. Maybe he'll get better."

"Maybe he won't," snapped Jinny.

Ben turned away from her. She thought he was crying. She couldn't remember him ever crying before.

This, she knew, was what she'd been waiting for, feeling in the world around her. This was the ominous cramp in her belly, the windless cliffs, the bleary sunrise. This was what her tugging had foretold—the world breaking to bits, the sky falling. She wasn't crazy after all. But she *was* to blame. This was her fault.

Ess pushed her way through the others, appeared at Jinny's side, and peered up at her bedmate, so limp and pale on the blanket. "Loo?" she whispered, reaching out to touch his arm.

"I don't think he can hear you, Ess," said Jinny, shaking

her head. "I don't think he can hear anything."

"Poor Loo," whispered Ess, watching.

Suddenly, it occurred to Jinny that in all the commotion, she hadn't helped Ess down the boulders, that she had run and stranded the girl behind after all that. "Ess? How did you get down those rocks? Who helped you?"

Ess gave Jinny a funny look. "Me!" she said brightly. Her voice was a sharp sound in the still room. "I did. You weren't there anymore, so *I* had to help me."

"Oh," said Jinny. It was all she could think to say.

"It's okay, Jinny," said Ess, looking proud, as she slipped a small hand into Jinny's.

That night, Ess wanted to stay with Jinny and Loo. And though Ben and Joon argued it was a bad idea, given what might happen in the night, Jinny shook her head. "You know what? She's not a Care anymore. Or she's not supposed to be, anyway. Ess is one of us. She's her own person, and she can decide."

"I want to stay," Ess insisted.

"Sometimes we have to do things we don't want to do," argued Joon.

"I *need* to stay," said Ess, as she sat down on the floor.

In fact, Jinny did not *want* to stay with Loo, herself. It was hard to look at his pale face. She didn't want to think about what might happen next either. She longed to curl up with Ess, to cuddle up and inhale the salty, dirty smell of her tangled hair as she slept, pretend that none of this was real. But Jinny didn't get to choose anymore. That time was gone.

After a while, Ess fell asleep, in the cushions on the floor, and Jinny sat on the edge of the bed, trying not to shake it, trying not to make things worse. Soon, she knelt down and pulled Abbie's letter from its hiding place. The room was too dark for her to read it, but she didn't need to. She'd memorized it by now. She whispered in the darkness.

"Dear reader who finds this, if I am gone,

"My name is Jinny.

"I lived here on this island.

"I loved it.

"I stayed.

"I held on."

Then, after a pause, Jinny added a line. She'd never be able to write it in ink, but it was there all the same, a ghost in the letter. As she slid the piece of paper into her pocket, she whispered it aloud.

"I held on.

"Too long. . . ."

25
A Direction

Jinny sat up all that night, in the darkness. Staring at the boy in the bed. Watching for any sign of change, anything but this stillness. Loo made no sound at all. Every few minutes, Jinny forced herself to lean over, touch his lips, make sure there was still a faint stream of breath passing between them.

The longer she sat, the more certain she became that this was the end, the very worst thing. Guilt and fear rasped inside her. Not even Ess's whistling snore could comfort her now. Jinny had broken a rule, *the* rule, and nothing had been the same since.

She had ruined the world. Unfortunately, that didn't mean *she* could fix it. The mist would knit itself back together, or it wouldn't. The winds would return to the cliffs. The snakes would settle. Or they might not. But she couldn't change those things. They were too big for her, beyond her. She couldn't undo them, or even understand them. She could only hope.

She looked down at Loo, so close to what had to be death, and she knew it was her fault. Each shallow breath belonged to her. He was her burden, because she'd claimed him and then failed him.

If Loo didn't wake up, she was to blame. But then what . . . what would they do *with* him? With his . . . body? Jinny couldn't even stand to think about it. . . . She watched Loo sleep without sleeping. Breathe without breathing. She watched him *be*. She watched him be *less* every second.

As the sun rose, Jinny began to shake slightly. Sleepless and hungry, she quivered. She was like a husk of herself, empty, hopeless, done. Then, in the half-light of early morning, she saw something peeking out from the shadows beneath the bed. She bent down, and laughed bitterly when she recognized what it was. She reached down and picked up . . . *mama*. It had been there all along.

"See, everything works out on the island," Jinny whispered. "Lost things always seem to turn up. Or they used to, anyway." Jinny reached over and set the grimy bracelet on the windowsill.

Loo groaned, almost inaudibly. He looked so small, so still. But even frail and dying this way, he made her angry. Underneath her guilt and fear, she was furious at him for coming to the island, changing everything. Even now, Jinny couldn't love him the way she loved Ess. But that didn't matter. It wasn't the time for Ess anymore. This wasn't about love, or what Jinny wanted. This was about what she owed Loo.

Jinny stood up. She wasn't sure what she was doing at first. Her mind couldn't fathom what her body had planned. She felt automatic, out of control. As though her bones—or some strange force inside them, stronger than her want and her fear and her doubt—took over. Standing beside the bed, Jinny stretched herself as tall as she could and gazed around at the cabin she loved. Then she stepped over Ess, leaned down, and scooped Loo up. Without word, without hesitation, Jinny turned, crossed the small room, and kicked the door open with a bare foot and strength she had no idea she possessed.

When Jinny stepped out into the chilly morning, she was alert. She didn't think she'd ever felt so awake before. Her skin tingled in the crisp air. However empty and tired she'd been just a few minutes earlier, however numb and lost, her feet wanted to move, and they knew the way. Jinny felt herself cutting across the beach alone, carrying her limp bundle beneath the smudgy sky. Past Joon, rekindling the fire. Past Ben, rousing himself in the kitchen. Both of them stared at her as she passed, eyed the child in her arms, but neither said a word. They turned to follow.

Then Jinny heard a shout. Many shouts. People were pointing up into the sky; and when Jinny looked up, she saw it herself. Something was falling, like sand. Sand from the sky. Only the sand was white and soft, and it fell slowly—landed cold on her shoulders.

"Snow," she murmured, and stopped walking. Jinny knew snow, from so many stories. She'd always wanted to see it. Now she felt it burn her face, her shoulders. It melted quickly on her skin, but the air was changing now too.

In a moment they were all there—all of them—trembling on the beach beside her. Staring up in wonder.

"Snow . . . ," said Sam. "It never snows." He looked amazed.

"It's cold," said Oz.

"We all know that," said Eevie.

Joon glared up. She said nothing.

"But do you think . . . is it a sign?" asked Nat thoughtfully.

Jinny spoke clearly. "It's only a sign if we read it," she said.

"I don't understand," said Nat, shaking her head. "What do you mean? What's happening to our island?" Her face was full of fear and wonder.

Jinny took a deep breath. "It's broken," she said in a clear loud voice. "I broke it."

The others turned to stare at her.

"I broke it when I didn't leave, and I'm sorry and I hope it can fix itself." There, she'd said it, at last, out loud. Loo was broken. Just like she was broken, and the island too. Nothing was the same, and it was all her fault. Now the sky *was* falling, as if she needed more proof. "'Nine on an island, orphans all . . . ,'" she whispered. Nobody finished the rhyme, but everyone was watching her.

Jinny looked down at the boy, cold in her arms. He was still sleeping, but barely. The breathless air was still coming from between his lips, but it was even shallower now. There was no time to waste. She began to walk again, faster this time, along the beach.

As she moved away from him, Ben called out to her. "But Jinny, we aren't supposed to move him. The book said. It'll hurt him."

Jinny didn't stop moving this time, or turn to look at Ben. She was done with delays. She only called out, up into the cold and swirling air, "I don't think there's anything that *won't* hurt him anymore."

Jinny kept walking. She *was* supposed to move him. For the first time in so many sleeps, she knew she was doing exactly what she was supposed to do. What she should have done all along. She did not want to do this. Not really, but it was her job. She would take him back, return Loo to the people who had sent him away, the other people who'd let him down. The people who had cast them all off. She'd take him back to his mama if he had one. To anyone who had answers and might be able to help.

Behind Jinny the others followed, nervous, unsure. Ess was there, Jinny knew. She could hear her crying. But she couldn't listen, couldn't stop. She had to keep walking now. It was only after Jinny set Loo gently in the boat that she allowed herself to turn around.

This was not a time for sweetness, for good-byes. She'd forfeited that sort of departure. That day had passed, long ago. This was a different kind of day. She turned to Ben. "I need your help," she said. "I can't lift the boat alone, not with him in it. Please?"

Ben stepped forward, and Joon did too. Together, the three of them lifted the boat, carried it to the water, and set it adrift. When the green wood hit the sea, it gave a shudder, as though it was waking.

"Jinny?" asked Ben.

Jinny had no time to answer him. She knew there was a world in all the things she should have told Ben by now. The Elder lessons she owed him, the feelings she'd buried, when he'd only wanted to understand. Probably apologies too. There was no time.

"Here," she said suddenly, reaching into her pocket. She pushed the crumple of paper into his surprised hand. "Ben, I'm sorry," she said. She couldn't explain, but maybe Abbie's letter would help. Maybe hers would too. They belonged to him now. They were his right. His puzzle. They were all she could manage.

Jinny turned away, to glance at Ess. When she did, she gasped. She remembered a fish, gutted on a sharp glinting knife, a small hand scooping the inside of the fish. That was how Jinny felt, staring into Ess's big eyes. She was gutted. She could almost feel the knife, feel something scraping everything that mattered out of her onto the cold sand. She bent down, knelt in front of the girl.

"I have to leave," Jinny said flatly. "I don't want to. But you'll be fine. I know it."

Ess shook her head wordlessly, wrapped her arms around Jinny's neck. "No," she cried. "It hurts."

Jinny hugged her back, and whispered into her hair, "That's what happens, Ess. Things hurt, sometimes."

"I don't want you to go," cried Ess.

"I don't want to go either," said Jinny. "But . . . there are more important things than what we want. Sometimes it isn't about us. Sometimes we aren't the center of the story. This is about Loo, now. Please, let me go."

Ess let go of Jinny and looked up into the older girl's face. Her tears were cold and her teeth were chattering. But she nodded and said, "Okay, Jinny. Okay," as Sam stepped forward and put an arm around her shoulder, curled her into a small hug.

Jinny stepped away, and it felt like something was tearing. Like *she* was tearing, and the very air was tearing around her. "Stay safe," said Jinny. "Be happy."

Ess nodded and wiped her snotty face on her shivering arm.

Jinny smiled sadly. Her last glimpse of Ess would be just

like her first. Snot faced and damp. "Good girl," said Jinny. "Good brave girl. Now go sit by the fire, get warm. Go." She made her voice firm, hard like stone. She carved out a last word. "Now!" and Ess turned away.

Jinny looked briefly at all the others, their serious faces trained on her, their eyes a mixture of sadness and bewilderment. This was all happening so quickly. But Jinny couldn't help that now. She didn't have time for each of them. She waved one hesitant arm in the air and turned her head quickly away. Then she stepped into the boat, which knew its way. Jinny envied the boat. It had only one task. One thought. To go. How simple that would be.

And that was just what it did—it went. It sped, away. In one quick moment, the boat took Jinny with it, breathless, suddenly gone. One minute she was on the island, and the next she wasn't. It was that easy.

As the boat picked up speed, charged out into the chilly sea, Jinny allowed herself to look down at Loo, beside her, nearly lifeless on the plank seat. She put a hand on his cheek. He was so small, so cold. She didn't love him, but then, she wasn't supposed to. He never should have been hers to begin with. Still, he needed her. And that need was a bond too, maybe even as important as love.

Jinny looked back up, and out, into the endless sea, the distance. She was trembling. She was so afraid. But she did not look back at the island. Not even once. As the sea spray mingled with the snow and fell against her skin, Jinny let herself tremble.

Staring out over the water, into the mist ahead, Jinny wasn't sure whether she was headed *home* or *away*, but she guessed it didn't matter. Either way, she was a girl in a boat, moving forward. Either way, there were waves all around her. Either way, the water on her face tasted like salt. And she was doing her best—that was all she could be sure of.

Somewhere out there, beyond the boat, was more. Jinny couldn't see it yet, but it had to be there. The alternative was too awful to imagine. So she decided she would believe in it. She would believe in it as hard as she could. Her future and her past were waiting. *Out there* were answers. She hoped she was ready for them.

"This only *feels* like an ending," Jinny said to the wind and the distance. And once she'd said it, she knew it was true.

What I Was Thinking About

AN AUTHOR'S NOTE

When I was working on the first draft of *Orphan Island*, I didn't tell anyone what I was writing about. I wasn't sure what I'd made exactly—if it was a bad book, a good book, or even a book at all. And while there were many differences between that first draft and what you're holding in your hands now, there was one big one: the book originally had a prologue. An origin story. The answers to many of the questions readers might have about the island, why it exists, and what everyone is doing there.

As you can see, that prologue did not end up in this book.

Since this book has been out there in the world, I've

thought about that prologue a lot. Because it turns out that some readers have struggled with the ending of *Orphan Island*. Some readers have been bothered by the questions I've left unanswered. Some readers might really want that prologue. So why isn't it here?

In order to answer that question, I'd like to tell you what it felt like when I was twelve.

I was a mess. It was a very hard year. My family was in flux, and for complicated adult reasons that I didn't fully understand, we had to move. I changed schools. I got my period. I started having complicated medical issues. This was the year when some girls had bras and others didn't, and some boys were mean to the girls and some boys were still our friends. Meanwhile I was in charge of my younger siblings all the time and they drove me crazy but I loved them, even though all I wanted was to be left alone (or for somebody to pay attention to me).

It was a lot, being twelve.

I felt caught in the middle of things, and confused, and annoyed, and clueless. More than anything, I was annoyed at my own cluelessness and how alone I felt in it. Nobody seemed interested in explaining anything to me. There were no answers—I didn't even know what questions I wanted to ask. But I could sense them. The questions. All around me.

This is the feeling I was hoping to capture in *Orphan Island*. In writing a book for my twelve-year-old self, I wanted, more than anything, to say, "It's okay that you don't know things. It's okay that you haven't even figured out all the questions yet. It's okay to feel unsure of yourself and yet still move forward. In fact, you have to. It's how you'll find the answers."

So you want to know what really happens at the end of the book? This is the answer: There *is* something on the other side of the mist. Of course there is. The little green boat will land on solid ground. But where it lands exactly depends on you. Because while an author begins a story, a reader always finishes it. *You* finish the story. You bring your own sense of the world to it, your particular thoughts, feelings, and questions. No two people read any book the same way.

So it's your turn now. Just like Jinny, you'll step forward into the unknown with imagination, hope, and resilience. Because, whatever path you imagine, the story only ever moves forward.

—LAUREL SNYDER

Summer 2018

Acknowledgments

Orphan Island took a long time to write and went through many drafts. As a result, a great number of people read excerpts and offered input over the years—so many that I'm afraid to attempt to name them here, for fear of leaving someone out. But I'm deeply grateful, and I hope everyone knows how appreciated they are.

That said, two wonderful wine-fueled late-night conversations stand out in my memory, and I'd be remiss if I didn't thank Christopher Rowe and Gwenda Bond, and also Brooke and John Marty, for helping me ponder world building, magic, and childhood. This would be a different book without them. Gratitude!

Ongoing love and thanks to my Atlanta gals, Terra McVoy

and Elizabeth Lenhard, who keep me working and laughing, answer ridiculous questions, and know when it's time to break for lunch. And to Rachel Zucker, who keeps me sane from afar.

A massive note of appreciation to Debbie Kovacs. When she asked what I was working on, and I responded that I wasn't so much "working" as taking bubble baths and staring at the ceiling, while pondering a mysterious island full of children, she replied, "That sounds like important work to me. Don't rush yourself." It was exactly the permission I needed at that moment in time, and it made this a different book altogether.

To Jordan Brown. An author fantasizes of an editor saying, "Do exactly what you're doing, only more of it." Working together on this book has been a dream come true, and I can't thank him enough for seeing where I was headed before I knew myself. His thoughtful precision and care have been a miracle to me.

To everyone else at Walden Pond Press and HarperCollins, many of whom I've yet to meet—including Danielle Smith, Patty Rosati, Viana Siniscalchi, Donna Bray, Amy Ryan, Renée Cafiero, Alana Whitman, Caroline Sun, Kristen Eckhardt, and Maya Haroutunian Myers. There's a kind of alchemy to bookmaking. A baffling process that somehow turns a story into a beautiful object, and then shares that object with the world. I am so grateful to all of you for your time, effort, intelligence, and magic. This book would not exist without you.

And to Tina Wexler, always and forever. Ten years ago, I signed on for an agent and got a friend for life. She reads *all* the drafts and talks me through my moments of doubt. I couldn't do this without her.

But most of all, thanks to my family. To my parents, for the very particular island they set me loose on. To Henry, Emma, Roy, and Susan, who shared it with me. To Mose and Lewis, for helping me find my way back. And to Chris. Who reminds me when it's time to get in the boat.

Such love!